MATCHED TO THE MERCENARY

SEEKING CURVES

HOPE FORD

JENNA

"What's his name?" John asks with fire in his voice. That tone probably works on other people but not me. Being his little sister, I've seen him cry over the commercials where the dogs are living in filth and need our help. So I know he's got a soft spot, and besides one of them being for neglected animals, the other one is for me.

"John, I'm telling you it's fine. I have it handled." It's the morning rush at Honeybee Coffee, the little shop I own in downtown Los Angeles. I bought it with the inheritance I received when our parents passed away. I would give it all back to have one more day with my mom and dad, but I know that's not possible. I'm working behind the counter, my phone tucked against my shoulder as I make up the daily coffees. We have quite a few regulars that get the same thing every day. At first I tried to upsell them or ask if they wanted to try new things, but they're not budging. So now when I see them walking by the big bay windows facing the sidewalk, I start their drink order.

"Handled? See, there is something going on!" My brother is pretty laid back, except when it comes to me. He's ten years older than me and has been out of the house for a long time. With me, he gets a little controlling and has to know everything I'm doing. It's sort of hard for him since he's stationed mostly on the East Coast now. But when our parents passed a few years ago, he started thinking that he needed to step up as a big brother. I don't want to complain, though, because quite honestly, I need him now more than ever. It's tough being in this world alone. But man he's funny when he thinks I'm keeping something from him.

I snort loudly into the phone and then start to openly laugh.

"What's so funny?" he asks.

"You. You're funny! You're getting all bent out of shape because you don't know something. I swear it must really bother you to know that you have intel on top secret missions for the country but you don't know who your sister is dating." I pause and then cringe when I think about my ex, Paul. "I mean, was dating."

"Was!" he screams into the phone. "See, I knew there was something going on. What did the asswipe do? If he hurt you... just a name, Jenna. That's all I need is a name."

I signal over to Madison, my best friend and manager of the shop, and point to the office door. She gives me a thumbs-up, and I leave her and the other two employees to deal with the rush while I go deal with my brother in the back.

As soon as I shut the door, I start. "John, listen, it's fine. We went out on a few dates. He was too controlling, I broke it off, and he didn't like that at all. It's fine. I'm handling it."

It's like I can hear his jaw tighten and his teeth grit through the phone. "What do you mean, controlling? What did he do?"

I know he's thinking all kinds of things. I'm sure in his line of work, he's seen the evils of the world and probably is thinking the worst. "It's not what you're thinking, bub."

His voice gets even grittier. "Tell me what I'm thinking."

Darn. I'm just going to have to tell him. Even

though it's embarrassing as all get out, it's nowhere near as bad as he thinks it is, I'm sure. Well, Paul is getting a little psychotic, but if I don't calm John down, it's hard telling what he'll do.

"Fine, listen, I swear you go from sweet brother to alpha military protector in an instant these days. Is all that ink from your tattoos going to your head or what?" I start to laugh at my own joke. I haven't seen John in a few weeks, but I'm sure he's already added more tattoos to his almost completely covered torso and arms.

John doesn't laugh or find me the least bit funny. "Quit stalling. I'm leaving on a flight soon."

"Oh no. I know you can't tell me where you're going, but I worry about you, John. Are you okay?"

Finally, he starts to soften. "I'm fine, sis. I have a whole crew at my back. You're the one that's by yourself in Los Angeles. I wish you'd come here. You would love it here."

Here we go again. He feels guilty for not being here when our parents were in the car accident and for leaving me alone here in the big city. I've thought about moving to Tennessee plenty of times. In Tennessee, I'd have my brother, but he's gone on missions more than he's not. "I'm not moving there to be alone. At least here, I have the coffee shop and

Madison. And don't say you could quit. You can't quit. I know what your work means to you."

He sighs heavily into the phone. "Tell me what's going on, Jenna."

Sometimes when I talk to him, he's the same laid-back brother I remember from my youth. Sometimes, like now, he sounds like he has the weight of the world on his shoulders, and I don't want to add to his stress. "Fine. I was dating Paul and—my gosh, this is so embarrassing—he didn't like what I was eating on our dates."

"Wait! What? He had a problem with what you ordered? That cheap bastard."

"No, it wasn't like that. He, uh, thought I needed to lose some weight and thought I should be ordering salads on our date."

The silence is deafening, and I can feel my face heat. This is so embarrassing. I've been overweight my whole life, but I love who I am and how I look. I'm definitely not going to stay with someone that doesn't feel the same. But still, it's an embarrassing conversation to have for sure.

"But, but you're beautiful just the way you are, Jenna."

I shake my head. I'm not so vain to say beautiful but ya know I'm definitely not going to argue with my brother. I never win when I do that. "It doesn't matter. It's over..."

"Yeah, I don't believe that. So when this dipshit said that, what did you do? Did you break it off with him? How did he handle it?"

I lean forward in the chair and put my head in my hand. Do I admit I gave him a second and third chance? It wasn't very smart on my part, but I'm chalking it up to being alone and needing male companionship. But at least I smartened up before I slept with him. That would have been horrifying. "Uhhh, well, after our third date, I did break it off with him and tell him I wasn't interested."

"And? I know there's more, Jenna. I'm your brother, I know you."

I barely resist rolling my eyes. "Well, he didn't like it. He thought—well, he couldn't believe that someone like me would break up with someone like him, so he's not really wanting to take the hint. But it's fine. Like I said, I can handle it."

"What's his last name, Jenna?"

Crap, I did let his first name slip. I shake my head. My brother works with men that could probably find out anything with a first name. "I'm not telling you his last name because it's done. It's over."

"All I need is a name, and I'll make sure you never see the dumb fuck again!"

"John! I don't want him killed."

"I'm not going to kill him. I'm just going to teach him a lesson."

"Okay there, killer, listen. It's not a big deal. I'm handling it."

There's a loud sound, and if I had to guess I'd say he's punching something. "But you don't have to handle it alone."

"If it was a big deal, you'd be the first person I called. You know that. But it's not a big deal."

"Jenna, I can hear it in your voice. I know you're not telling me everything."

I clench my eyes tightly and feel bad for lying, but I don't want him to go onto a mission while he's worried about me. "I promise. You know everything. I'm fine. Now quit worrying about me and start thinking about your next job. I want you focused, John. I need you to come back in one piece, please."

He doesn't say anything for the longest time. I'm worried he's going to keep pressuring me, but he surprises me. "You don't want me to worry? Fine. Do something for me."

"Anything," I blurt out.

"Seeking Curves."

It's just two words, but it's enough for me to wish I hadn't agreed to do something for him.

"John, come on..."

"I'm serious, Jenna. If you were with someone that was good to you and took care of you, I wouldn't have to worry."

I throw my hand in the air in frustration. He may not be able to see it, but it makes me feel better. "First of all, I'm a grown-up. I don't need someone to take care of me. Second of all, is this really my brother? The same guy that used to threaten boys in high school for just talking to me?"

"Yeah, but I'm not there anymore." He pauses, and when he starts again, his voice is thick. "Jenna, I can't lose you too."

And just like that, he has me. I can't argue with that. I don't even want to. I worry about the same with him. I can't lose him. If me signing up with Seeking Curves gives him peace of mind, I'll do it. "What do you even know about this place?"

"You fill out a questionnaire. They ask everything. Then they guarantee a match. It's all legit. I had one of the tech guys here look into it."

I sigh loudly into the phone. I may agree to do it, but I don't have to be happy about it. With everything with Paul going on, I really don't want to date, but I'm not going to deny John. "Fine. I'll do it."

"Today? You'll do it today?"

I roll my eyes and grumble. "I'll do it today. I promise. Now no more worrying, okay?"

He sounds breathless, almost like he's jogging. "That's great, sis. I'm about to be late for a meeting. But promise you'll call me if you need me. Even if I'm not in town, I can get someone to you..."

I interrupt him before he starts to go through the line of people that would help me and start giving me their phone numbers again. "I promise. I have all the numbers saved in my phone. I'll call if I need anything. I love you, bub. Take care of yourself."

He blows out a breath. "I love you too. I'll call you when I can."

I lay my cell phone down on the desk in front of me and clench my eyes shut. I know my brother's going to be okay, but it's always hard when he leaves for a job. Plus, everything with Paul—well, it's just too much to deal with right now. Plus, now I have to sign up for some dating service? Ugh.

I should probably get back out front, but instead, I lay my head down on my arms and try to collect myself.

2

DYLAN

*A*ll eyes are on Nash at the front of the room. As a commander for our group, he gets respect from every one of us, and all eyes are on him. "All right, guys, this is an in-and-out situation. Our intel tells us that there's an unprotected path once we get there. The bad thing about it is getting there. We'll fly into Brazil, then have to take a boat. The last leg of the trip will be on foot. It will probably be a few days of walking, but it's nothing you haven't done before. Once you have the target, you'll walk to the designated meetup—just a few hours north. Jaxx will be there to transport home. Everyone clear?"

I nod, ready for this mission. I get a thrill any time the team is called on an assignment. I know we're needed and can do things most people can't. We are the last hope for most people in these dire situations, and I love being part of it. Even though a lot of times, I'm serving my part of the mission from a computer, I know my part is important. I get intel and keep the guys safe. I couldn't think of a more important job. These guys depend on me, and I take it seriously.

I look around the room of guys that are more like family. I don't know if it's because I never had a family of my own and was in and out of foster care homes more than I care to count or what. But these guys are my family. I'd do anything for them.

Bear and Knox get up first and walk out of the conference room first, while Nash talks in the corner with Walker, Knox, Aiden, and Bobo. John, who goes by Knuckles, is sitting in the same spot at the conference table, staring at the phone in his hand. He obviously has something on his mind. It was noticeable when he was almost late to the meeting. No one is ever late for a meeting that Nash calls. I close my laptop and walk toward the door, stopping next to him. "You okay, man?"

He's worried. That much is clear by the way he's lost in thought. "Look, man, if you're worried about this assignment..."

He shakes his head. "I'm not. Can I talk to you?"

I nod. "Sure, man. Want to go to my office?"

He rolls his head, flexing the muscles in his neck. So he's not just worried. He's pissed too. "Yeah, sounds good."

He follows me to my office, and I shut the door behind him. He's pacing the room, and I sit down at my desk, setting my laptop to the side. I watch him quietly and wait. John is a good guy and has been through the wringer the last few years. Even though he's considered a player, even more so since the death of his parents, he always puts his sister and our team first.

He finally stops and gestures at me. "Are you going on this trip?"

I shrug. The plan is for me to stay here, but plans change. "I can go."

He shakes his head and takes a step toward me. He's completely on edge, and I'm not used to this side of him. "What is it? Just tell me."

He points at my laptop. "Can you do your job from anywhere?"

"For the most part. Sometimes it's easier when I have my three monitors, but this assignment I can do from anywhere."

He's nodding his head and starts to pace again. I stand up and block his path, and he looks shocked to see me even standing in front of him. Did he not hear me get up? He's not focused, and whatever's bothering him is going to get him killed in the field if he doesn't fix it. I hold my hands up in front of him. "All right, listen. What's going on?"

"I have a big favor to ask. Huge, actually."

I nod. "Whatever, man. You got it."

He laughs and shakes his head. "No, really. It's big. I mean, I can pay you."

I try not to get offended that he's offering to pay me for help, but I have to admit it does rub me the wrong way. "I'm not taking your money. Tell me what you need."

"Someone is messing with my sister. An ex-boyfriend. She's not telling me the whole story." He starts to pace again, and I just listen as he continues. I walk over to my desk and start packing up my laptop and everything else I need. "She does that when she doesn't want me to worry, and she's especially close-mouthed since I'm about to leave on a mission. But she's the only family I have left... If something happened to her..." He stops mid stride. "What are you doing?"

I put my headset into my bag. "I'm packing." I

sit down at my desktop computer and open the search window to start searching for a flight. "Los Angeles, right?"

He leans forward and puts his hands on the desk. "You're going? Just like that? What about Nash?"

I keep typing. "I'll talk to Nash, but with this mission, I can work from anywhere. It will be fine."

I find a flight that leaves in two hours. It's not much time, but in this line of work, I've learned to pack fast, and since we've already been briefed on the mission, I should have plenty of time. I complete the purchase button. "Done."

He stands up and crosses his arms over his chest. "Done? Just like that?"

I pull out a notepad. "Yeah, John. Just like that."

"Most people call me Knuckles..."

I shrug. "I like John better... now tell me about your sister."

He finally sits down across from me. "Jenna Taylor, she's twenty-five, she owns Honeybee Coffee in downtown Los Angeles. She lives in an apartment, and it's not the best part of town. I tried to convince her to move, but she just recently bought the coffee shop, and she doesn't want the extra expense right now. And before you ask, I've tried to give her money, but she won't take it."

"Okay, she's independent," I say while I write that down. "What do you know about the trouble she's in? The ex."

He smacks his hand down on the desk in frustration. "Nothing. His name is Paul. I've had a tendency to be a little protective of her, and she doesn't tell me a lot about any guy she dates."

I write down the name *Paul* with a question mark. "Okay, what does she look like?"

I'm looking at the pad in my hand, waiting for the description when my phone pings. I look up, and John is holding up his phone and then pointing at mine on the desk. I open the message app, and instantly my whole world changes. John's sister is beautiful. She has long brown hair that is fanned out over her shoulders. Her big brown eyes are looking back at me, and I swear it's like she's looking into my soul. I feel a jump in my chest, and without thinking, I bring my palm up to my heart, but I still can't take my eyes off of her. Her body is curvy, and all I want to do is put my hands on her hips and...

"Hey, uh, so Riggs, this is starting to get a little awkward. That's my sister."

I bring my gaze up to John and realize what I'm doing. I gulp, and my voice cracks when I tell him, "She's very pretty."

He's watching me closely, but at least he doesn't look mad. "I think so. Too bad Paul didn't think so. I swear I could punch him right in the face."

I lock my phone and lay it down. "What do you mean?"

"I don't know the whole story, but what I'm getting is he didn't like the way she looks, and she broke up with him. Now, he's got some kind of issue with her breaking up with him." He stands up again and starts to pace. "I don't know, Riggs. This might be all a waste of time. I may be reading more into it then I should be."

There's no way I'm not going. He can change his mind, but I'll still go. Now I need to know she's all right. "I'm going." I stand up and finish throwing things in my bag, and I put my phone in my pocket.

John whips his head around, no doubt at the tone in my voice. He's watching me closely, and I wait for the threat. I wait for him to warn me about keeping it all on the up and up. But he doesn't. "You'll like Jenna. Everyone does. And I think she'll like you too." He walks to the edge of the desk and stands toe to toe with me. "All I'm saying is keep her safe and don't hurt her. Can you promise me those two things?"

I let out a long breath. I thought for sure we were about to have a problem because if he warned me away from her, I was going to have to tell him no. "I promise. I'll keep her safe, and I won't hurt her."

I shake his hand that he's holding out and then walk past him. He stops me as I get to the door. "Thanks, Riggs. I appreciate you doing this for me."

I nod. "Be safe on your mission. You know how shit gets fucked up if you're not focused. Keep yourself alive. I don't want to tell your sister you're dead."

He smirks. At least he gets my humor. "You got it."

I walk out with a whole new purpose. I resist taking my phone out and looking at Jenna's picture again. I have to talk to Nash and then I have a plane to catch. I'll have six hours in the air to come up with a plan on how to make her mine.

3

JENNA

It's a new day. That's what I keep telling myself, anyway.

I did what I promised him. I signed up with Seeking Curves yesterday afternoon. They had an option to do it all online, and it was very convenient. All in all, it took me thirty minutes to complete, but they asked everything. I mean everything. Some of the questions are still making me blush. Oh well, my part is done. I did what I said I'd do; the rest is up to the company. It won't bother me if they don't call me back.

I've been anxious ever since yesterday when I got off the phone with my brother. I am every time I know he's on a mission, but even more this time. I don't know if it's because I know he's worried about me when he should be focused on the job or what, but I'm concerned.

The morning rush at least helped me get my mind off things, but now that it's over, I'm back to worrying.

"I've never seen him before."

I look over at Madison, who is wiping the front counter off. She gestures with her head to a man in the corner. He's watching us, and when Madison and I both look at him, he bows his head and starts typing on his laptop. "Me either."

I keep watching him. There's something about him that intrigues me, but it could just be the fact that he's handsome. His hair is brown with gold highlights. Natural looking. He doesn't look like the type of guy to get highlights in his hair anyway. He's obviously tall, and the way his long-sleeved Henley fits across his chest and arms, he's built. He grabs his cup of coffee, and when he raises it to his lips, his eyes meet mine.

I swallow... hard. I don't want to look away.

"Uh, dibs. I saw him first," Madison says jokingly.

I pull my gaze away from him and back at Madison. My face is hot because I got caught drooling over the stranger. I definitely am not in a position to start dating. Not until I get this thing with Paul handled. I wouldn't have signed up with Seeking Curves if I hadn't promised my brother. "Sure," I mutter. Even the words don't taste right. I get a sick feeling in my stomach about it even.

I work the rest of the morning and into the lunch rush, keeping an eye on the man. He's working, obviously. Sometimes he's trained on what he's doing, completely focused, and it seems a bomb wouldn't get his attention. Other times, he's sipping from his Honeypot glass.

With my back to the counter, I'm making a special Honeybee latte with milk, cinnamon, honey, turmeric and vanilla when Madison stops next to me. "Forget it."

I finish stirring the concoction and turn back to the counter, handing the frothy drink over. "Forget what?"

Madison has no filter and doesn't seem to care that people are standing around. "You're up. The stranger wanted nothing I was offering."

I roll my eyes. "Quit calling him a stranger like there's something forbidden about him being here or something. We're in Los Angeles. We're not going to know everyone that walks in the door." I give her the side eye as I hand the change over to the last customer in line. As soon as he walks away, I can't help but give Madison a hard time. "And what exactly are you offering him? Because I'll have you know I run an upstanding business here. We don't offer s-e-x."

She snorts and starts laughing. Which wouldn't be that big of a deal if she didn't have a laugh like a cute hyena and then hollers out, "Sex."

I shrink away from the counter and look. Sure enough, the sexy stranger is looking our way. I pull Madison behind the tall part of the booth. "Are you kidding me? Did you have to scream s-e-x for the whole shop to hear?"

She rolls her eyes. "Do you always have to spell sex?"

I shrug my shoulders.

She puts her hand on her hip and gasps. "Oh my God, you do! Say it, Jenna. Say sex or I'm screaming it again."

I can feel the heat racing up my neck and onto my face. I know Madison, and sure enough, if I don't say it, she's definitely going to scream it. "Sex," I say calmly, and by now, my face is as red as a ripe tomato. Damn my pale skin.

Madison just laughs it off. "Good, now go and see what the stranger is doing here."

I try to act like I don't care. "How do you know he wasn't interested in you?"

"Because everything I asked him was a no, and he kept looking at you the whole time. Not once did he make eye contact. He's definitely interested in something, but it's not me."

"Did you offer to refill his coffee?"

"He's not drinking coffee. He's drinking water." She rolls her eyes. "Who comes to a coffee shop and doesn't drink coffee? Plus he's been here"—she holds her wrist up to look at her watch—"for almost six hours."

I start to walk away. "Maybe he needs the Wi-Fi. What's the big deal? He's not hurting anyone."

Madison growls. "He could hurt me anytime."

My shoulders tense, and my heart misses a beat. There's that feeling again. Why do I feel so territorial about this man? I peek around the opposite edge of the counter, and it's like he's looking for someone on the other end. Madison's head appears over mine, and she starts to whisper, "See, he's looking for you. Just go talk to him. Ask him if he wants another cinnamon roll. He devoured the one from this morning."

"Fine," I mutter.

I say fine, but it takes me another ten minutes to

get the nerve up to go and talk to him. I grab a pitcher and fill it up with fresh ice and water. I put on my best smile and walk toward him. When he sees me, he sits up straighter, closes his laptop, and watches me. His gaze burns a trail down my body and back up again. I sometimes hate being the center of someone's attention, but with him, I don't. *Oh my God, Jenna, why are you swinging your hips?* My hand with the pitcher starts to shake, and I switch it to my other hand. Nerves are making me crazy, and just when I get next to his table... I walk right past him.

Shaking my head, I pick up some trash off a table and throw it away before walking along the wall to get behind the counter. I don't stop until I'm behind the tall side of the booth, and only then do I let out the breath I was holding.

"What the fuck was that?" Madison asks in a loud whisper. Her eyes are wide as she's staring back at me. I'm waiting for her to start making fun of me, but the look on my face must be stopping her. She honestly looks as freaked out as I feel. "Are you okay?" she asks me.

"I can't do it."

She shakes her head. "Why not?"

I shove the water pitcher into her hand, and

thankfully she catches it or else it would fall to the floor. "I literally couldn't stop. The way he was staring at me. My God, the man is hot, capital HOT."

She sets the pitcher down. "That's right... staring at you. He's stared at you all morning. Don't let what your dumbass ex said about you make you start to second-guess every good-looking guy out there."

I'm still shaking my head.

"Jenna, you don't have to marry him or anything."

Still I'm shaking my head.

Madison grabs me by the shoulders. "Jenna, you are a successful, beautiful, kind-hearted woman. You obviously like this guy, and he can't keep his eyes off you. Obviously there's something there. And if there's not, so what? You're not asking him out or anything; you're literally asking him if he wants a refill. Nothing has to come of it if you don't want it to."

I stare wide-eyed at my best friend. She's right. I know she's right. I also know that everyone needs a Madison in their life because she's always pumping me up and even helped me deal with Paul when it all went south.

She keeps nodding her head. "So you know what you need to do?"

I gulp. "I need to go talk to him."

"Excuse me," someone says from the counter.

Madison rolls her eyes. "Yeah, I'll be right there," she tells the person and then gets right back in my face. "All right, now do it. Just ask him if he needs a refill. That's it. See what happens."

I nod, and finally Madison releases me. She gives me a stern look before going to help the customer.

I can do this. I can do this, I tell myself over and over as I pick up the pitcher of water. *You're just asking a customer if he wants a refill. No big deal. You can do this.*

I walk around so I come at him from the back this time. I watch the muscles move in his neck and shoulders and then his body tense when I get close. *You can do this, Jenna.*

I stop next to his table and am holding the pitcher with both hands to stop myself from spilling it, but at least I get the words out. "Can I get you a refill, sir?"

4

DYLAN

*T*he coffee shop was closed when I got off the plane last night. Instead of checking in at my hotel, I went straight to Jenna's apartment. I made a point to walk the complex, making a list of everything I needed to do while I'm in town. More lighting in the parking lot, security cameras on her floor. And I'm not sure, but if I had to guess, she doesn't have an alarm in her apartment or any on her first-floor windows.

I did what I could through the night, but the ones in the apartment will have to wait until she lets me inside.

I didn't lay eyes on her until she came in to work this morning. I was already sitting in my rental car parked across the street. She was looking down at her phone the whole walk to the front door, not a care in the world. Anyone could have come up on her.

And I'd kill whoever it was.

I don't know what it is, but before I even heard her voice, I knew that she's the one. The thought that someone may want to hurt her or has hurt her has me completely on edge. I won't stop until I can claim her as mine.

I wasn't able to find anything more on the ex-boyfriend, but it's obvious just from the little bit I've overheard from being in the coffee shop all morning, there's definitely something going on. And from the way Madison talks, it sounds like she would want to be in line to take care of him. Of course, she'd have to get in line after me.

I've watched Jenna all day. Well, I watched her while I also worked. The guys in Brazil needed an alternate route once they were on the ground. I was able to access the satellite layouts and found them another way in. I've kept one earpiece in, just in case I'm needed, but for the most part, I've kept my eyes on Jenna.

She obviously doesn't realize how beautiful she is. The number of men that come in here and flirt with her—well, I've lost fuckin' count. Each time a man approached her, I was ready to shove him out the front glass window. *She's mine, fuckers!* I scream it over and over in my head, but I don't say a thing out loud. If I did, there's no doubt I'd scare the woman half to death.

She and her friend don't know what to think about me. I've caught them both watching me and then whispering. I'm sure it's because I've sat in this same spot for six hours, unless you count the few bathroom breaks I've taken. Other than that, I've stayed at this table.

The friend, Madison, came to talk to me earlier, but I didn't look at her. I didn't want to. I only have eyes for Jenna, and there's no way I'm going to fuck it up by talking to the friend. So I grunted, "No thank you" at her offer of a refill, and then she turned and walked away. If you ask me now, I wouldn't be able to tell you anything about what she looked like. Ask me about Jenna, and I'd tell you that she has brown hair that is thick, and I can't wait to wrap my hand in it. Her lips are puffy and pink, full and perfect for kissing. When she's nervous, she fidgets. When she sees something she wants, her eyes get round, and she bites her lower lip. That's the exact look she gave me when she walked by here a few minutes ago.

Now she's standing here asking me if I want a refill, and I'm reveling in the fact that she called me sir, thinking I wish I was somewhere private with her, and all I can do is stare at her dumbly.

She bites her lip, unsure. "Ummm…"

I barely resist reaching for her and soothing my thumb across her lower lip. "Yes. Yes, I'd love one."

She nods and pours the water into my glass. Her eyes switch back and forth between the cup and me. "Can I get you anything else?"

There's a thousand things I want from her, but nothing I can say to her now. "I'm Dylan. My friends call me Riggs."

I thought about it for the whole plane ride, and I knew that I just needed to be up front about it all. Under different circumstances, I could protect her without even talking to her. But that's not an option. I watch her closely, wondering if she will make the connection. I've known her brother for years. How the hell I haven't met her before now is beyond me.

Her forehead creases, and she blinks. "I'm sorry. Do I know you?"

Yes. I'm your future husband. That's what my head says, anyway, but I know I can't say it out loud. I clear my throat and decide to just put it out there. "Yeah, well, sort of. I work with your brother."

Her face crumples right in front of me. In place of the soft smile, her expression is filled with terror, and the pitcher of water in her hand falls from her grasp. I barely catch it before it hits the floor. "Is he okay? Oh my God, did something happen to my brother?"

Already there are tears forming in her eyes, and I regret the nonchalant way I mentioned her brother. He said she always worried about him, but I didn't expect this. There are so many things going through my mind right now, but the most important is fixing what I just did to her. I set the pitcher on the table and grab Jenna by the shoulders. "He's fine, Jenna. I've been talking back and forth with him all morning. He's on a mission in Brazil." I shake my head. All the years of training and experience go right out the door when it comes to Jenna. I'm not supposed to disclose locations. "I wasn't supposed to tell you that. He's on a mission, but he's safe."

She wipes at her eyes, searching my face to see if I'm lying to her. "I promise. I wouldn't lie to you."

She pulls back from my hold. "How do I know that? I don't even know you."

I point to the chair across from where I've been

sitting. "Please, sit down." She shakes her head. "Please. I'll prove to you that you can trust me. Just give me a few minutes."

She has so much mistrust on her face it kills me. She's obviously been hurt, and there is real fear in her eyes. I hold my hands up, my palms facing toward her. "Please," I plead with her again.

She nods, still frowning, and pulls the chair out across from me. I slowly take my seat and put my hands on the table in front of me. The ear device I have on is still live in case they need me, but it's been quiet for around an hour. No doubt the guys are making their way to the target.

"Has your brother ever mentioned me?"

She shrugs. "I think so." She obviously doesn't want to answer any questions. She wants to be the one asking them. "What's my brother's nickname?"

I nod in understanding. So this is how this is going to go? I don't care; I'll sit here all evening if it means I get to talk to her. "Knuckles. But I refuse to call him that. I call him John."

"How did he get that nickname?"

I try to hold my smirk in. She wants to know if I am who I say I am, but obviously she's never been told how her brother got the nickname. Oh well, I'll tell her, it's not state secrets. "He likes to fight. He may carry knifes, guns, whatever... but the man likes to bare knuckle fight."

She looks horrified for just a minute before clearing the expression from her face. "Okay, how many tattoos does he have?"

I laugh. "Too many to count."

She's staring back at me, searching for a question, so I decide to help her out. "He's been with the team since he left the army five years ago. You're his only family, and he would do anything for you."

She shrugs, like duh, all this is obvious.

"He has a scar on his arm that he covered up with a tattoo. He tells everyone he was in a knife fight but actually he fell out of a tree when he was kid."

She leans forward. "He told you that?"

I nod, grabbing for the glass of water to keep from grabbing for her. I knew it was going to be hard to keep my hands off her, but I didn't realize it would be this hard. She's even more beautiful up close. "Yeah, one night after a mission. We, uh, had both been drinking."

She's starting to believe me. As a matter of fact, I'm sure she already does, but if this is a game she wants to keep playing, I'm in. It doesn't matter to me. I have nowhere to be but right here.

She crosses her arms over her chest, and it pushes her breasts up even further. The V-neck of her shirt hints at cleavage, and my mouth waters as my cock starts to lengthen in my jeans.

She lifts her shoulders in a shrug. "You could have found that out from hospital records, whatever."

I shift in my seat to make room for my hardening member. It's time to end this back and forth. "Do you have your phone on you?"

She nods and pulls her phone out of her apron. "Okay, I'm assuming that John sent you numbers in case you ever needed to get a hold of him."

She nods again.

"Great. Search Ghost 3."

Her eyelashes flutter as she looks down at her phone. Her eyes widen when she opens the contact. "Call it," I tell her.

She starts shaking her head. "I'm only supposed to call if..."

"Call it," I tell her again.

She rolls her eyes and pushes the call button. Before she can even put the phone to her ear, my phone on the table between us starts to ring. I pick

it up and hold it out for her to see. The caller ID
says *Jenna Taylor*. It pains me to know she's been in
my phone all this time. She's been right there... and
I didn't know. One thing is for sure—I'm not going
to waste any more time.

I look at his phone and then at him. He has my name in his phone. I have his number in mine. Holy crap!

"Wait! If John's on a mission, why are you here? Why didn't you go? I thought you all went together on these things."

I feel euphoria, like I've stumped him and won some kind of game we're playing or something. I'm smirking, knowing I've one-upped him but also trying to figure out why I'm fighting this so hard. He's obviously who he says he is.

"I'm the tech guy. I go on a lot of the missions. The ones I don't I can do from anywhere. Well, anywhere with Wi-Fi or hotspots so I can access satellites and the VPN..."

He keeps going on about tech stuff. No doubt he sounds super smart, but I can't seem to take my eyes off his lips as they move. I barely notice he stops talking before he catches me staring at him, and I jerk my eyes back up to his. There's laughter in his face, and the thought that he knows I'm attracted to him and he finds it funny doesn't sit well with me at all.

"So why are you here? Did John send you?"

He sighs. "Yes. I'm here at John's request."

He wants to say more. It's on the tip of his tongue, and I wait, but he presses his lips together firmly.

"Okay... so why did he send you to Los Angeles?"

He shifts in his seat. "He told me about Paul."

Oh my God! He didn't. Oh but no, I can tell he did by the pity I see on Dylan's face. I put my hand to my forehead. "What exactly did he tell you?" I ask, enunciating each word. *I'm going to kill my brother. I told him I had it handled.*

Dylan shrugs. "Just that you had an ex giving you problems."

I put my hands firmly on the top of the table and stand up. "Well, I'm sorry he sent you all the way across the country. You can go home now. I'm fine."

He covers my hand with his own. I try to pull away, but it's no use. He lifts my hand, stands up, and tugs me toward him.

"I'm not leaving, Jenna. I won't leave town until I know that the ex is no longer going to be a problem. We can do this the hard way or the easy way; you get to pick."

"Uh, hey, mister, you got a problem?" Madison asks, shoving herself next to me and pointing her finger into Dylan's chest.

He is pissed. It's obvious by the throb of the vein in his neck and the stare he gives Madison. He looks at the finger she's poking in his chest, and images of him snapping her finger in two or something crosses my mind. Isn't that something these specialized military men are trained to do? I'm sure even the smart tech guys have to know how to fight.

I grab Madison's finger to stop her. "No, there's no problem. Dylan was just leaving."

"I'm not leaving," he says, getting Madison riled up again.

He holds his hand up in front of Madison. His other one still has a death grip on mine. "I'm not leaving until I know Jenna is safe. I was sent here by her brother to take care of the ex. If Jenna wants me to leave after that, I will."

My heart starts to hammer in my chest. *Do I get a choice in this? Is he saying he'll stay?* I shake my head. *Get it together, Jenna. That's not what he meant at all.*

Madison lowers off her tiptoes. "Wait, John sent you? You're a friend of John's?"

Dylan is back to staring at me, so he nods his answer.

Madison slaps him on the shoulder. "Cool. I hope you do take care of Paul. He's a dumbass."

And with that, Madison walks off to go back behind the counter. Thank goodness it's getting later in the afternoon, and the coffee house is almost empty before the after-work rush starts. After looking around the shop, I lean my head back to look up at Dylan. He's still holding on to my hand, but now his free hand is on my waist. Being this close to him touches all my nerve endings and makes me feel like my body is about to short circuit. It's almost electrifying being held by his hands.

"You don't have to do this," I tell him.

He releases me and pushes his hand through his hair. "Do what?"

I shake my head and put my hand on my hip. "Do you know how crazy it is that you flew across the country for this? It's not that big of a deal. I. Can. Handle. It."

He points to the chair. "Sit down."

When I don't move, his voice softens. "Please?"

His eyes are pleading with me, and he did ask nicely, so I sit down and clasp my hands on the table. "Fine. I'm sitting."

He sits back down across from me and pulls out a pad of paper. "What's Paul's last name?"

I stare back at him. Are we really doing this? I shake my head. "You're not going to give up, are you?"

He doesn't even hesitate. "Not until I talk to Paul and know he's not going to mess with you."

I lean in and whisper, my eyes searching the coffee house before finally landing back on his. "You're not going to kill him or anything, are you?"

"That depends on what he did to you." He says it point blank and with a completely straight face.

I was joking. I never thought he would kill him. "Dylan, you can't kill him."

His hand tightens on the pen he's holding. I watch and wait for it to bend and break under the pressure, but it doesn't. "Are you still in love with him?"

I snort. Loud and obnoxiously before covering

my face with my hand. "I'm sorry."

He's not laughing. His eyes are searching mine. "Do you love him?" He seems almost panicked to know the answer.

My hands drop back to the table. "I went on three dates with him. No, I don't love him. But I also don't want him dead."

He flexes his shoulders and rolls his neck. "What did he do to you? Then I'll decide if I'm going to let him live."

Here we go again. It was hard enough telling my brother over the phone. It's going to be even harder, face to face, saying it to Dylan. "Well, I broke up with him after, uh, I found out he wasn't really a nice person, and he couldn't believe that *I* could break up with *him*," I tell him, stressing the *I* and *him*.

He grits his teeth and nods. "And?"

I roll my eyes. "And he didn't like it."

"What did he do?"

I sigh in frustration. "Well, first he started coming by my apartment. Which wasn't a big deal; I just didn't let him in. Then he started screaming through my door at me. I called the police, and they have been regularly patrolling the area. I haven't seen him there since."

He leans back and crosses his arms over his chest. For just a second, I get preoccupied with the flex of his arms. He has really big arms for someone that does computer work. "Uh, and then he started coming here making rude comments. I'm getting random phone calls from blocked numbers, on my cell and here at the shop. And then—" I take a deep breath. "Then my car window was busted out. There was a picture of me, in my apartment, half clothed. He stuck it to my steering wheel with a knife, and it had writing on the picture. It said... It said, *Fat bitch! You will pay.*"

I try to act like it doesn't bother me. I've long moved past the point where other people's opinions matter to me. But it's still embarrassing. All of it is. The fact he got that picture, what he wrote on it, breaking into my car. The whole thing makes me feel violated.

Dylan's tone is harsh. "How did he get the picture?"

I lift my shoulders. "I don't know. I didn't give it to him, if that's what you're asking. And I'd never pose in my underwear. All I can think is he put a camera in my apartment. I've searched everywhere, and I can't find it. But I've been sleeping on the couch because it still freaks me out."

He's staring back at me, and I can feel the rage coming off him. I start to squirm in my seat. I don't want Paul dead, but I also don't want him to bother me anymore. I didn't admit it to John because I didn't want to bother him before his mission, but I have been scared. "Are you going to kill him?" I ask, half joking, half not.

"I'm going to stop him. He won't mess with you again. What's his last name?"

"Stevens. He works at Johnson and Schuster Accounting. He's a senior accountant there."

I wait for him to write it down, but he doesn't. He puts his laptop in his bag. "When do you get off?"

I look at the big clock on the wall. "I can leave anytime. I just saw Story walk in. And the night manager should be here soon."

"Story?" he asks.

I nod. "Yeah, she works here. That's her name."

He nods, rolling his shoulders again. "I need to check in with the team. I need your car keys so I can check your car. Then I'm going to drive you home and check the apartment."

"Dylan, you don't have to."

He reaches for my hand and holds on to it. "I do have to. Neither he nor anyone else is going to mess with you again. Do you have the knife and picture?"

A warmth spreads up my face. It wasn't the most flattering picture, and I really don't want to share it with him. "I do. Why do you want it?"

"When I find the camera in your apartment, I'm going to track the signal to his computer or wherever he's saving the images. I'll need the picture and knife for the police."

I pull my hand back, shaking my head. "This is already mortifying to know that someone is watching me and for you to see me like that; now you're telling me everyone at the police station is going to see me naked?"

He grunts and shakes his head. "Do you trust me, Jenna?"

I shouldn't. I just met him, but I'd be lying if I said I didn't. "Yes. I trust you."

He reaches across the table and palms my shoulder. "This is what I do for a living. No one will see the picture or any videos of you in a compromising position. No one will see you like that, I promise."

I nod. "Except for you?" I ask breathlessly.

His eyes are locked on me. "Except for me. I'll have to scrub the video before I turn it over. I'll have to watch it to remove the parts I don't want people to see."

Oh my God, Paul is a bigger asshole than I thought. If I was a more vengeful person, I'd wish him dead at this point. "And once you do that—scrub the video if there is one—no one will see me—uh, see those?"

"I promise you, Jenna."

It's all too much. It's like I'm being violated. "Okay."

He didn't expect me to agree. Hell, I didn't expect to either, but he has a good plan, and he's right. He does this for a living. I'm just going to have to trust him, no matter how hard that is.

I get up. "So car keys, picture, knife? They're in my office. I'll be right back."

I walk off, and I can feel his eyes on me. Madison is watching me closely, and I ignore the way she's wiggling her eyebrows at me as I walk past. I'm sure Dylan sees her doing it, but I can't worry about that. Now I just have to worry about my brother on a mission overseas, my ex-boyfriend going psychotic, and then Dylan looking at probably nude video or pictures of me. Oh yeah, no big deal. I'll just breathe and get through it.

6

DYLAN

I take the keys and the manila folder that I assume holds the knife and the picture from her before going outside. Besides needing to check out her car, I also need a breather. Being this close to Jenna is hard. I want to touch her, hold her, kiss her, and there's no way she's ready for that. She's freaked out... and she should be. Especially with everything she has going on.

I put the manila folder in my bag and walk out to her yellow convertible bug. I can't help but smile when I see her car. It suits her. I put on gloves and open the car doors and the trunk. I grab the electronic bug sweeper from my bag and work from one end of the car to the other. It's clean.

I close up the car and walk back to the shop.

Constantly, I'm surveying the area, looking for anything or anyone that may be out of the ordinary. When I walk back in, Madison points me to the office door, and I knock on it before opening it.

What I see has me dropping to my knees next to Jenna. "What is it? What's wrong?"

With her head still down, and her voice muffled, she asks. "Did you look at it?"

I take my hand and start to rub her back. I don't know what happened from the point I left to go outside to now, but I'm not having it. Whatever upset her, I'll take care of it. "Your car? Yes. No tracking devices. What happened?"

She lifts her head, but half her face is still covered by the smooth strands of her dark brown hair. "No, not my car. The picture. Did you look at it? Because if you did, I'm probably never going to be able to look you in the eye again."

I can't resist running my fingers through her hair. I tuck the long strands behind one ear and force her to look up at me. "Jenna, I'm a professional. When I look at your picture it will be for pure investigative purposes, that's it. I promise you."

She rolls her eyes. "That doesn't make me feel any better."

I blow out a big breath. Time to be honest with

her. "Look, I'll admit, I'm attracted to you." Her eyes widen, and when she starts to shake her head, I put one hand on her chin to hold her still. "I'd be lying if I told you I don't want to see you." I clear my throat. My cock is already pressing against my zipper just thinking about it. "But the way those pictures were taken, well, I wouldn't do that to you. I'm going to only compare the angle of the picture to the angle of where I find the camera. That's it. I'll give you the picture back. I'm going to scrub the images from the device in your apartment and wherever they're hosted at. That's it."

She still isn't comfortable. It's obvious, but I don't know what else I can say to make her feel all right with all of it. I hate that this Paul did this to her. I expect her to argue with me or try to talk me out of looking at the camera images, but she doesn't. She surprises me when she sits up. "You're attracted to me?"

Fuck, I want to kiss her. I could do it too. Prove just how attracted I am to her. But she deserves better than that. I know she does. And that's the only thing stopping me at this point. I stand up, pulling her from the seat. I put one hand on her shoulder and the other at the base of her neck. I lean down, so we're eye level. "Yeah, I'm attracted to you. And if we didn't have this thing with Paul and the fact that your brother sent me here to protect you... well, I'd show you."

She wants me to kiss her. The way she's looking at me, she might as well be begging for it. I want to. Fuck, I want to. But I don't. My need for wanting to do things right by her is overwhelming, and I won't allow myself a kiss. Maybe because I know it won't stop with just one kiss. No, I'm not doing this until I have things settled with her ex and talk to her brother. After that, there's nothing that will stop me.

I lean forward and pull her to my chest. I bury my nose in the top of her head, breathing in the scent of honeysuckle and sweet vanilla. Her arms go around my waist, and I hold her there, not wanting to let her go. Because I can't resist, I press my lips to the crown of her head. She inhales deeply, her body trembling against mine. Right now, she probably thinks I'm a sweet guy. But I'm not. I'm far from it. I've done things that will haunt me for the rest of my life. I'm thinking about all the things I want to do to her, and every image is of her naked while I hold on to her hips as I move in and out of her. Yeah, I'm not a good man. But she makes me want to be better.

I rest my cheek on her head. "Are you ready to go?"

She mutters yeah, but she doesn't move.

I smile. "Can I take you to dinner before we go to your apartment?"

And just like that, I can feel her walls coming up. She pulls from my arms. "Can we order a pizza or something? I'd convinced myself that the picture was taken from a window or something. But now, the thought of a camera... well, I just want it out."

She's shaken up, and soon she'll know that whatever she asks of me, I'll do for her. "Absolutely, let's go."

I follow her out of the office and stand to the side while she says goodbye to Madison, Story, and the night manager. When she's done whispering with Madison, I hold her hand and walk her out the front doors. "This way."

She stops and jerks me to a halt since I'm holding her hand. "My car is over there."

I rub my thumb across her wrist. "I know where your car is. We're going to take mine. I'll bring you back in the morning."

"Dylan."

"Jenna," I say right back.

She turns her head to the side. "I can't ask you to..."

"You're not asking me. I'm doing it." I shrug, knowing I should probably sugarcoat it or something. "I'm taking you home. I'm sleeping on your couch and then I'm bringing you back to work tomorrow."

She stomps her foot, and all it does is make her look even cuter than she already does. I try to hide my smirk. "I may have to go out tomorrow, but I'll have someone watching you here at the shop."

"No, Dylan."

"Yes, Jenna. I just found you, and I'm not going to let anything happen to you. Let me do this my way."

Her mouth falls open. That's around the third time that I've tried to let her know that something is going on here. She can try to ignore it if she wants, but this, the two of us, it's happening.

She finally nods, and with her hand still in mine, I start to pull her toward the rental car. *Now all I have to do is make it through the night without making a move on her. Surely, I can do that.*

7

JENNA

*A*s soon as we got to my apartment, I sat on the couch while Dylan worked. He brought in bags of equipment from the car and instantly went to work. There was a recording device in my bedroom. I don't know when Dylan looked at the picture I gave him, but almost immediately when he got into the room he was able to find the camera, and I'm assuming it was because of the angle of the picture. The camera is so small, it looks like it was just a random marking on the wall. He deactivated it and put it in his bag. He then went around the rest of the apartment, checking for recording devices. He put new locks on all the windows and installed an alarm system at the door and all the windows. "Uh, is all that necessary?"

He continues to work. "Yeah, anything that's going to ensure your safety is necessary."

He moves through the apartment working in a strategic matter. It's obvious he's done this before. It makes me wonder if he and the guys do this for a lot of women.

When a knock sounds on the door, he's out of the guest bedroom where he was working at in the living room in an instant. "I got it."

I stand up and grab my purse to get my wallet, but before I can even pull the bills out, he's already shutting the door and carrying it to the kitchen. "I can at least buy your dinner. Especially after everything you've done."

"Thank you. I appreciate that, but I pay when you're with me."

"Well, thanks for dinner."

He stops from pulling out the small white containers. "What? That's it?"

"What do you mean?"

"You're not going to argue with me?"

I open the silverware drawer. "Fork? Or do you want to eat with chopsticks?"

"Chopsticks."

I close the drawer and grab napkins and drinks. "Why would I argue with you? You're obviously a gentleman. I'm assuming you're old school."

He holds my chair out for me. "Old school? Is this your way of saying I'm old but you're just too nice to come out and say it?"

I side-eye him as I sit down in my seat and he pushes me in. "No, what I'm saying is that chivalry isn't dead with you." I gesture to the seat I'm in. "You hold out seats, open doors, hold my hand to cross streets, you buy my dinner. You're a good guy, Dylan Riggs. Your mom raised you right."

He pauses, opening containers, and then sits down heavily in his seat across from me. "I'm not a good guy, Jenna. I've done things, bad things that I can't go back and change even if I wanted to. I don't want you to get the wrong idea about me. And I guess while I'm being upfront about everything, I didn't have a mom. At least not one that raised me. I went through eleven foster homes before I aged out and found myself in the Army and eventually with your brother's team." It sounds as if he's talking about the weather instead of important things about his life. He puts some of the chicken lo mein on my plate and then some on his own. "And I'm not really old school... I don't know, maybe I am. I'm not doing those things because they're habit or anything like that. You make me want to do those things. I want to do them... for you."

I stare at him with my mouth hanging open and my fork gripped in my hand. He just keeps going. "Crab rangoon?"

I nod, and he puts two on my plate. When I look down, my plate is piled high with something from each of the containers. He's not eating. He's staring at me, searching my face, and I know he's wondering what I thought about all his confessions. I set my fork down and reach for his hand. I meant to only touch the back of his, but he turns it and intertwines our fingers together. Another tremble goes through me. I've never had a man that liked to touch me as much as he does. I like it... I like him. "You're a good guy, Dylan. You can try to convince me otherwise, but everything I've learned about you today tells me that you're a good guy." I clear my throat and try to work up the nerve to say what I want to say. No guts, no glory. "I like you."

He gives me a lopsided grin and squeezes my hand. "I like you too."

We sit at the dining room table and eat with our chopsticks while we talk about any and everything.

Well, not everything. He makes it very apparent that there are things he won't be able to tell me, and I completely understand. I've heard the same spiel from my brother before.

"Can you tell me anything? The guys you work with? Where you live, anything?"

He shrugs. "Yeah, sure. There's quite a few of us. We're all ex-military."

I shake my head. "But I thought John was in a branch of the military now."

His eyes widen. "Well, we are sort of on our own. We do things a little differently, but ultimately we have the same goal."

"To help people?" I ask.

He nods. "Yeah. There's Walker; he is the backer of the whole operation. He owns half of Whiskey Run, the Distillery, and the headquarters."

"Where exactly is the headquarters?" I ask as I take a bite of the egg roll. A bit of the juice rolls down my chin, and without even thinking about it, Dylan leans over and uses his thumb to wipe my chin before sticking it in his mouth and licking it clean. Heat flares in the pit of my stomach. I couldn't imagine anything hotter than that right there.

"Whiskey Run. It's a small town, but there's a

lot of land that goes between there and Jasper. Our headquarters are on the outskirts of town, surrounded by a bunch of ranches."

I nod. "And the rest of the guys?" I'm enthralled by it all. Already I've learned more from Dylan than my brother ever would tell me.

"Nash is our commander. Great guy. Then there's your brother, Jaxx, Bear, Bobo, Knox, Colt, Cash, and Houston. We're somewhat of a rough bunch, but they're all good guys."

I nod, seeing the pride on his face as he talks about them.

When we're done eating, we take turns in the bathroom showering. He insists I go first, and when I'm done, I sit on the edge of my bed with the bedroom door wide open. It's right across the hall from the bathroom, and after fifteen minutes, Dylan comes out in shorts and nothing else. My mouth drops as I watch him towel dry his hair and then loop the towel around his neck.

He catches me watching him from my spot on the bed. "You okay? I know today was a lot."

My face heats, and I try to cover up my reaction to him with the first thing that comes to mind. "Have you heard from my brother? Is he okay?"

He nods. "I talked to the team while you were

in the shower. He's good. If all goes as planned, he'll be back in the States in a day. Two max."

I let out a breath. "Good. That's good. So are you sure I can't take the couch? You'd probably fit better in the bed."

He grunts and shakes his head. He takes a step into the room and stops. "Come here."

I don't know why I question him, but I do. "Why?"

"Because I want to talk to you."

I sit straighter on the bed. "Why can't you come here and talk to me?"

My God, is that my voice? It's low and seductive sounding. I didn't even know I had it in me.

"Because if I come over there, I won't stop with talking to you. I'll have you naked underneath me before you can count to two."

My heart stops. It's just a few beats I miss, but it definitely happened. I unfold my legs and climb out of the bed. The walk across the room feels like a mile instead of just a few feet. "Okay," I mutter when I'm standing in front of him.

He has his hands gripping the edges of the towel that's hanging around his neck. "Talk to me."

"Nothing, I'm fine."

"Something's bothering you. I can tell."

I blow the hair out of my face. "I don't want you to get in trouble."

His eyes widen. "Get in trouble? For what?"

I twist my hands together in front of me. "I think we should just call the police and let them handle this. If you're anything like John, which I'm assuming you are, then you're not going to be able to resist putting your hands on Paul." I shake my head and look up at him. "I just don't want you to get into any trouble. That's all."

His hand goes to my cheek and brings my face up so I'm looking at him. "I'm trained—"

I interrupt him. "I know you're trained to do this but—"

He laughs. "I'm sorry, Jenna, but there's no way I'm turning this over until there's a solid case. I'm not going to risk him getting away with it on a technicality. And yes, I'm probably going to put hands on him. But anything I do, he deserves it."

I nod and tilt my head farther back. The longer we've stood here, the closer we've moved. It's like there's an invisible force bringing us together. He's staring at my mouth, and I lick my lips as I go up on my tiptoes. I've never wanted someone to kiss me more than I do right now.

Right when I'm sure it's about to happen, I hold

my breath in anticipation, and he releases me, taking a step back into the hallway. "Go to bed, Jenna. I'll see you in the morning."

Humiliated, I reach for the door and shut it before practically running to the bed. Maybe I'm getting this all wrong, but if this is some kind of game to him, I don't want to play anymore.

8

DYLAN

I fucked that up. I'm pacing the living room, replaying what I said in my head and realizing just how badly I fucked it up. What is it with me? You'd think I'd never dated a woman before and instantly I know. I may have dated before, but I've never felt this before. Not for another woman and definitely not to this extent. I could barely focus on my job today. And nothing I say or do is coming out right.

She doesn't understand. I sit down on the edge of the couch and pull out my phone, pulling up her contact information. I send her a text. *Hey.*

Almost immediately the message shows as read. I wait, holding my breath for her response.

The bubbles that indicate she's typing pops up...

disappears and then pops up again. Finally, the message comes through. *What?*

I smile at her sassiness. I love that she doesn't put up with bullshit. Even mine. *I'm sorry.*

The reply is instant. *You have nothing to be sorry for.*

I do though. I feel like a teenage boy around you.

Her response is a question mark.

Fuck, how do I say this without being crass? How do I tell her that all I can think about is sleeping next to her, holding her, and making her mine? *I can't control myself around you. I want to kiss you.*

She sends a laughing emoji. *I would have let you.*

My hands start to sweat, and I lay the phone on the coffee table in front of me and stare at it. I wipe my hands up and down the front of my shorts before picking the phone back up. I type as I walk down the hall to her bedroom. One kiss. That's it. I'm going to give her one kiss. *Did you lock your door?*

No.

I pocket my phone as I push her bedroom door open. She's lying in bed with the covers up to her chest. As soon as I walk in, she sits up, and the sheets fall to her abdomen. Her silky top is tight against her breasts, and my eyes are drawn to the hard peaks. She's staring at me with desire on her face even though she's trying to hide it. She doesn't know that her body is betraying her. With her hard nipples, ragged breaths, and flared nostrils, she's wanting this just as badly as I am. Her eyes follow me across the room, and I walk up beside the bed and sit down on the edge. Looking at her brings out the most possessive feelings I've ever felt. I put one hand on the bed next to her and the other on the headboard next to her head. I should ask her first, but I'm not going to. "I'm going to kiss you now."

I press my lips to hers, and a collective gasp comes from both of us. I lift my hand to the base of her neck, turning my head so I can deepen the kiss. I may have told myself one kiss, but there's no way I can stop once I've started. We're testing each other, gentle nips that turn into hungry, open-mouthed mating of our lips. The kiss takes my breath away, but I'll go without as long as I have her mouth on me. Her hands slide up my abdomen, and her touch scorches my skin. I gasp at the same time as she whimpers, and I pull away. I have to before I take this too far, too fast.

I jump up from my seat on the bed and bend over, hands on my knees as I try to catch my breath. My cock is hard and swollen, and as I look at her with her wide eyes, freshly kissed lips, and mussed hair, it takes everything I have to not climb into bed with her.

I stand up, doing my best to ignore the painful throb of my cock. "I'm going to the living room. Sweet dreams, baby."

She's speechless as I walk across the room. When I have the door almost shut behind me, I tell her, "Lock this door."

I shut the door firmly behind me and walk into the living room. I sit down on the edge of the couch, and I can't get the kiss out of my head. I knew we would be good together, but I didn't know we'd be molten.

I lie back on the couch that she put a sheet over. My head hits the pillow, and I'm surrounded by the smell of honeysuckle and vanilla. A scent that is purely Jenna. I sit up, grab my bag, and get out my laptop. I know I'm not going to be able to sleep, so maybe I should try and work.

I start compiling information on Paul. The sooner I get the matter resolved, the better. I hate thinking that he's been watching Jenna, but I'm going to handle it. I run his criminal history, his credit history, all the jobs he's worked at, everything. I search it all, taking notes as I go. Everything I discover about him causes me to have more questions. Finally, when I've found all the information I can on him, I move on to the camera that I found.

I pick up the camera tag and know I should start scrubbing it, but there's no way I can do it tonight. My body is still reeling from having Jenna in my arms. I can't look at images of her right now. It wouldn't be right. It's going to be hard enough to rein in my attraction to her; now it's just too much.

I lie back down on the Jenna-scented pillow and roll to the side and inhale deeply. It's so late now, and I'm exhausted, so I have no trouble falling asleep. When my eyes drift closed, I grin, knowing that I'm going to be dreaming of the curvy woman that is sleeping in the next room.

9

JENNA

We're back at the Honeybee, and it's a rush this morning. I've already had a cup of coffee, but I'm thinking I might need another. I barely slept last night after that kiss. And when I did, it was not a sound sleep. I tossed and turned all night, my body never really coming down from the high of being in Dylan's arms.

I was hoping for a repeat this morning, but it didn't happen. He held my hand the whole way here, but once we were inside the shop, he locked himself in my office and went to work on his laptop. I know he has work to do, and his is more top secret than mine, so I offered him my office, and I've been working at the counter all morning.

When there's finally a lull in the madness, I

check my phone. There's a message from Dylan. *I talked to your brother. I told him you were worried so he said for you to call him when you're not busy. He's back in the States.*

I reply with a thank you and tell Madison I'm taking a break. I freshen up my cup of coffee and walk to a booth and sit down. Dialing my brother's number, I smile when I hear his voice on the line. He sounds tired, but he sounds good. "Hey, sis."

"Hey, yourself. Are you back home?"

He pauses. "Well, I'm back in the US. I haven't made it to Tennessee yet."

"But you're fine, right? No injuries. You're good."

He laughs. "You worry too much. I'm good. How are you? How's everything with you?"

"I swear, big brother, if I wasn't so worried about you, I'd probably be giving you a piece of my mind right now."

He's not scared in the least. "Oh no! Not a piece of your mind."

"Har, har! Funny, tough guy. I told you that I had this thing with Paul handled. You didn't have to send Dylan all the way here. You have to start treating me like an adult. I'm not a kid anymore."

He's silent, waiting for my tirade to stop. After a

moment of silence, he asks, "Are you done now?"

"I could go on."

His voice deepens. "And I have half a mind to come straight to Los Angeles. Dylan told me about the camera. Paul is a dirty bastard, and he deserves what he gets."

I sigh. "I don't want you or Dylan to get in trouble for this. I think we should call the police."

"This is what—"

I interrupt him. "Yeah, I know. I heard it from Dylan last night. This is what you all do. But I still don't want you to get hurt because of it."

He changes the subject, and it's not one I'm ready to talk about—especially with him. "Last night? Did Dylan stay at your apartment?"

I'm nodding my head. "Uhhh, yeah. He slept on the couch. He didn't want to leave after finding the camera."

"Man, I'm going to owe him for this."

I hit my hand to my head. Why didn't I think of that? "I didn't even think, John. I'll pay him. I can just imagine what it's costing you—the flight here, rental car, and he's missing work. Tell me how much, I don't even have a clue what you guys make for things like this. I'll pay him."

"You're not paying him, Jenna."

"He's helping me. Why can't I?"

"Uh, because he won't even take money from me. He's definitely not going to take it from you."

I stare at my office door that's still closed. "Wait? You're not paying him?"

"No. He refused to take money. He said he wanted to do it. I even tried to wire him money to cover the airfare, but he has some kind of block up on his account and refused the wire transfer."

I shouldn't ask. I definitely shouldn't let my overprotective brother know I'm interested, but I can't stop myself. "So why would he do all this? It doesn't make sense. Is he really just a good guy that likes to help out?"

"He's one of the best guys I know." My whole heart feels his words. It's a big compliment coming from my brother. "I have thoughts on why he's doing it, but why don't you ask him?"

My curiosity is piqued now. I grab my coffee mug and head back toward the counter. "So am I going to see you soon, big brother?"

"I'll be that way as soon as I get a break in jobs. I'm about to reboard the plane. I gotta go."

"Okay. Be safe. I love you, John."

"I love you too, sis," he tells me before hanging up the phone.

I hold the phone in both of my hands. I have so many questions now, and the only one that can answer them is on the other side of my office door. Just as I get to the counter, my phone dings, alerting me that I have an email.

I click it to open it, and it's from Seeking Curves. I cringe, realizing that I've completely forgotten about signing up for the matchmaking service the other day. I scan the email quickly. *Thank you. Yada, yada. We received your application. Guarantee a match. We're running you through the system, and we'll be sending you your matches soon.*

I sigh in relief. Great. I have time to tell John I changed my mind. I may have promised him I'd sign up, but I can't imagine going on a date with anyone now that I've met Dylan.

Before I make it to the office, Madison stops me with a hip check.

"So? Spill it."

"Spill what?" I ask her.

She grabs me by the arm and moves in front of me. I have nowhere to look except right at her. She searches my eyes, and her face lights up like a kid on Christmas morning. "What happened last night? Did you have s-e-x?"

I gasp. "No!"

I try to pull from her grip, but even with how tiny she is I still can't budge. "You did, didn't you?"

Finally, I give up struggling. "I did not. We kissed, but that was it."

Her smile drops. "But you wanted to have s-e-x."

There's no denying it. I'm sure Madison already knows the answer by the dopey smile I've had on my face all morning. But there's no way I'm going to admit it to her. She'll never let me live it down. There's no stopping Madison. So I stand here and talk to her about my insane attraction to the man that I just met yesterday.

Dylan

I'm on edge like I've drunk ten coffees when I haven't even touched one. At some point I'm going to have to tell Jenna that I don't like coffee, but that's going to have to wait for another day. I've been holed up in her office all morning. I've been meticulously scrubbing hours of video, blurring the images of her body. It seems I was worried for nothing. I had thought I wouldn't be able to contain my body's reaction to seeing her, but one look at the innocent look on her face and knowing that this piece of shit violated her with these videos, all I could see was red. Once I finished the videos, I continued on my search of everything I could find out about Paul. Just when I was about to stop, I hit the jackpot. I hooked into the Wi-Fi printer in Jenna's office and started printing everything I needed. I made a few phone calls, and I'm about to gather my stuff when there's a knock on the door.

"Come in."

Jenna pokes her head around the door.

I stand up and pull her into the office. "Why are you knocking on your own office door?"

She shrugs. "I didn't want to interrupt you."

I start putting my computer and papers into my bag. "I'm about to leave. I have a few things to take care of, but there's someone watching the place. If you have anything out of the ordinary or anything you need, just call me."

"Are you coming back?" she asks, and I stop packing to look at her.

"Yes. I'm coming back, but I don't know how long I'll be. When you're ready to go, you can leave anytime. My friend, Charlie—" I pull my phone from my pocket and scroll through my photos before holding up an image of an old Army buddy that is helping me out. "This is him. He knows to stay low-key. You won't even know he's following you unless you need him. He's going to follow you home and will stay in the parking lot until I get there. All I ask is when you leave, please go straight home. I trust this guy, but I don't want any surprises. Okay?"

She nods, and I know I've overwhelmed her. She opens her mouth to say something, but nothing comes out.

"Go ahead. Say it."

She shrugs and shakes her head. "It's nothing. Maybe we can talk about it when you get back later."

I look at my watch and then back at her. I have to go, but I hate to leave her. I put my bag over my shoulder and pull her to me. I pull her too roughly, the adrenaline of what I'm about to do already rushing through my body. A puff of air comes out of her mouth as she lands hard against my body. I put my forehead to hers. "This is all going to be over tonight, Jenna."

Her eyes widen, and something flashes across her face, but just as fast, it's gone. I press my lips to her forehead. "I hate to go, but I have to."

She nods, clenching her eyes tightly together. "I know. Just be safe, okay?"

I smile softly at her. She has no idea that this mission is simple compared to others I've been on. Well, simple in the physical sense. In an emotional sense, it's probably been the hardest. I know I'm going to have a hard time not permanently damaging this fool, but all I keep telling myself is that I'm not going to be good to anyone if I go to prison. Right now, I don't have the backing of the Ghost team behind me. This is not a Ghost mission. This is now personal.

I drive across town and park across the street of Paul Stevens' small house. I wait only a few minutes before an unmarked police car parks in front of me. I get out at the same time he does. We stand next to each other, both of us looking up and down the empty street. "Are we good?" I ask him. I got his number from Charlie with the promise I could trust him. I hope he was right.

"That depends. Did you bring me what we talked about?"

I hold up the manila envelope. "It's all here. Evidence of him laundering over a million dollars from the accountants. Illegally obtained footage from him that connects to an ISP at this address.

Images, account numbers, paper trails... everything is all there. Everything."

He holds his hand out for the transfer. "And you don't want credit? You've recovered a million dollars. You don't want anything?"

"I want fifteen minutes with him before you arrest him. That's all. Then he's all yours."

The officer rubs his hand across his mustache. I can read people, and he's not comfortable with my request. "How did you get mixed up with this? What's he to you?"

I tilt my head to the envelope he's now holding. "The woman in one of the videos is my woman."

"Fuck! Is he going to be alive when you're done with him?"

I grit my teeth. I know this is the right way to do this. "He'll be breathing."

He pauses for just a second before holding his hand out. "Deal."

I put mine in his. "Deal."

As soon as I let go, I'm walking up the steps. I'm going to fix this. I'm going to make him wish he'd never met Jenna. He's going to spend the rest of his life in prison. And I may leave him with breath in his body, but he's going to wish he was dead.

10

JENNA

The rest of the afternoon went by at a snail's pace. I kept checking my phone, thinking that Dylan would call. I almost texted him, but I didn't want to bother him if he was in the middle of something. When it was time for me to go home, I walked out to my car, looking everywhere for this Charlie that is supposed to be following me, but I can't spot him anywhere. I drive straight to my apartment, walking slowly through the lot, keeping an eye on my surroundings like Dylan talked to me about, but still no Charlie. It's only after I get to my apartment and look out the window that I find him sitting in a dark grey sedan with his eyes locked on my window. I wave stupidly at him, and he just lifts his head with a nod.

I feel a little better that someone is here, but I'd feel a lot better if it was Dylan. I go through the house, straightening up things, doing a load of laundry, and taking a shower. And he's still not here. I turn on the TV but can't concentrate, so I turn it back off.

Every car light that shines through the window as people pull into the parking lot, I jump up and peek through the blinds. Now it's starting to get dark, and I find myself pacing the living room. Finally, another car pulls into the lot, and before I even see it, I know it's him. I know it's Dylan. I look out the window, and sure enough, he's getting out of his rental car. He walks toward Charlie, who's been sitting there all evening, and then starts walking toward the apartments. I open the door before he gets to it. As soon as his eyes meet mine, a rush of emotion hits me right in the chest. I don't even let the poor man in before I'm bear-hugging him and sobbing against his chest.

His arms come around me, and his hands rub up and down my back soothingly. He walks me into the apartment, using one hand to lock the door behind us. He pushes the hair back, and with his hands cradling my face, he searches my face. "It's okay. You're okay."

I try to pull myself together, and he uses his thumbs to wipe the tears on my cheeks. "Hey. Don't cry. I hate seeing you upset like this."

"I was so worried."

"Jenna, I'm not going to let anything happen to you. You have to know that."

I shake my head. "I wasn't worried about me. I was worried about you."

He looks shocked at my claim. And it all starts to fall into place. He came from foster homes. The only family he's ever known is probably the army and my brother and the rest of the guys. He doesn't realize that if something happened to him, I'd be lost. I grip the front of his shirt in my hands. "I don't want to lose you, Dylan."

He seems at a loss for words, and he pulls me in, tucking my head under his chin. His voice is thick with emotion. "You're not going to."

I don't know how long we stand here, but slowly his body starts to relax. I pull away reluctantly but reach for his hand because I don't want to break all connection.

As soon as I do, he flinches, but he doesn't pull away. I turn his hand in mine, and his knuckles are busted, with the skin torn. I gasp and reach for his other hand. Sure enough, it's hurt too. "Dylan. You're hurt."

He laughs then. "You should see the other guy."

I stomp my foot and walk toward the linen closet where I keep the first aid kit. "This isn't funny. You're bleeding."

He's following behind me. "Jenna, this is nothing."

I stop with the kit in my hand. "You're hurt. It's something, all right. And it's all because of me."

I point to the kitchen table, and he sits down without any argument. I look at both his hands, shaking my head. "What happened?"

I use gauze and alcohol to clean out his cuts. The sting, and I know there is one, doesn't even seem to faze him. His eyes are on me, but I'm concentrating on his hands. "Paul was arrested. I found enough to put him away for a long time."

I lift his hand and point at his injuries. "And this?"

He shrugs. "I wasn't going to let him go without knowing the mistake he made. He'll never bother you again."

I finish cleaning his hands and put liquid Band-Aid on the cuts that need it. "Can I ask you something?"

"You can ask me anything."

I busy myself cleaning up the wrappers and getting up and throwing them away. "Why are you doing this?"

When he doesn't answer right away, I turn to look at him. He's watching me but doesn't say anything. He points at the seat I just vacated. I go back and sit down. He pulls me toward him where my legs fit between his. He is leaning forward, his hands resting on the outsides of my thighs. "Why am I doing this?" He pauses. "Why am I helping you? Is that what you mean?"

I nod because talking is not an option right now. The intimacy of being this close to him is going to my head.

"Because your brother asked me to."

I nod. I don't know why I thought his answer would be any different than that.

He leans forward, his hands moving farther up my hips, and his fingers dig into my skin, holding me. The hold is a possessive one and makes ripples through my body. "Your brother asked me to help, but as soon as he showed me your picture, there was nothing that would have stopped me from coming here and meeting you."

I put my hands over his. I don't try to stop his

hold or anything, I just need that connection. "John said you wouldn't let him pay you, and I have a feeling if I offered to that would offend you."

He nods. "Yeah, it would. I wouldn't take money to protect you, Jenna. From the first time I looked at you on my phone over two thousand miles away, I knew you were mine to protect."

I shake my head. "But..."

He stops me. "No. You're mine, Jenna."

His words send a tremble through my body. With way more confidence than I've ever felt before, I lock eyes with him. "Prove it."

His body jerks as if he was given an actual physical blow or something, but he acts fast. He stands up, pulling me with him. His hands go around my waist, and he lifts me up into his arms as if I weigh nothing. My legs go around his waist and my arms around his shoulders. His kiss is overpowering. It's like he has something to prove as he stalks down the hallway to the bedroom. He stops next to the bed, and he groans as he pulls his lips away. "I need you."

I cup his face, wanting his lips back on mine. "You can have me."

He grunts as he sets my feet on the floor. He

pulls his shirt up over his shoulders and lets it drop to the floor. His muscles flex as he moves, and I can't wait to feel his weight over me. He sits down on the edge of the bed. "Strip for me."

I'm already shaking my head, and he leans forward and touches my abdomen, bunching the material of my T-shirt in his hands. "If I do it, this will be over quick. I want to take my time with you. Strip for me, Jenna."

I've never undressed in front of a man in my life. I'm more of a hide under the cover kind of girl, so when Dylan asks this of me, my first instinct is to tell him no. Watching him lean back on his arms, his dark eyes watching my every move, it's intimidating. But what gives me the strength to do it is the obvious bulge in his jeans. I look at it. He's hard and erect, and he cups himself through his jeans and shifts. He wants me... and he wants to see me.

I pull down my shorts and step out of them. Then I quickly remove my shirt. I should probably worry about looking graceful, but I'm not. It's more like when you're trying to rip off a Band-Aid; you do it quick. When I'm standing in front of him with my matching black bra and panties, I have my fist clenched at my sides.

His voice is deep and thick. "I want to see it all."

Goosebumps raise on my arms. But there's no way I'm not going to give him what he wants. He looks at me like he would give his last breath to have me, and I'm not going to let him down. I reached behind me and unclasp my bra, pulling it down my shoulders and letting it fall to the floor. Then I put a finger on each side of my hips and pull the panties down my legs, letting them fall to my ankles. I kick them off into the corner of the room. When I'm completely naked, I take a huge deep breath and then look at him.

His stare is like a caress as he looks down the length of my body. I squirm under his watchful eye. A need like I've never felt before starts in my belly and tugs.

He stands up, and it's like every muscle in his arms and chest are vibrating. He reaches out and brushes the hair back that is covering my chest. His gaze is replaced by his hands as he cups my large breasts and kneads them. My head lolls back as his thumbs move across the hard, peaked nipples. My inner thighs are wet from the pleasure and anticipation that rocks through my body.

When his hot lips latch around my hard peak, I

gasp. I wasn't ready for the sensation that bursts from that one simple touch. With his mouth on me, his hand slides down my abdomen across my stomach and to my mound. My hips jerk in eagerness. I need him to touch me there.

His fingers plunge into my core, stroking through my slick swollen folds. My hips rock, seeking pleasure from him. When he finds how wet I am, he groans. It's a guttural sound that echoes in the room.

In an instant, I'm flat on my back in the bed, my knees raised up and hooked over his shoulders as his tongue probes my swollen sex. He torments me, pushing me to the edge and then bringing me back. Over and over until I'm half out of my mind, and finally, I put my hand on the back of his head and hold him to me. I lift my hips, seeking the pleasure from him, and he doesn't disappoint. He sucks my clit into his mouth, working his tongue across the bundle of nerves until complete ecstasy takes over and my body is nothing but a writhing, thrashing uncontrolled mass of limbs.

Through hooded lids, he stands up, and I watch as he quickly pulls down his jeans and underwear. His cock is hard, leaking cum from the tip. I lean up, and my legs are shaking like Jell-O, but there's no way I won't taste him right now. I wrap my hand around his pulsating girth, and his hips buck. I stroke him and watch as his whole body flexes. If I didn't know then, I do now. I have way more power over Dylan than I thought.

Dylan

SHE'S STROKING ME, and already I'm about to come into her hand. She raises up, her big breasts shaking as she cups my balls and licks the tip of my cock. I about come right here and now. She opens her mouth, and she's so far gone, I know she'd take my cum and swallow it without a second thought. But that's not where I want it. I want to shoot my seed into her womb; I want to paint her channel with my cum, leaving no doubt that she's my woman now and forever.

I push her backwards, and her legs automatically fall open. I put my knee on the bed and climb the length of her body, feeling her hard nipples stroke against the hair on my abdomen and chest. When we're face to face, I kiss her, putting everything I have into that kiss. I pull away, searching her eyes. "I don't want to use anything."

Her fingers play with the hair on my chest, and I stop her by covering her hand with my own. I'm too close to losing control. "Are you clean?" she asks.

I nod. "Yeah, I'm clean."

She lifts her head to kiss me lightly. "Me too. And I'm on the pill."

I grimace because that's not what I want to hear. I want her thick and swollen with my babies, but there's time for that. One step at a time. I wrap my fist around my cock and line up at her center. Slowly, inch by inch, I move inside her, giving her time to stretch to my girth. She grunts, a sound that comes deep in her chest, and when I'm fully seated, I hold completely still. My brow is wet; every muscle in my body is stretched and pulled tight. I'm barely holding on because the need to move is overwhelming. Slowly, I start to pump my hips. With the taste of her pussy on my lips, I move in and out of her. I'm pushed with an urgency to have her.

Her fingernails dig into my back, her cries become louder, and I can't stop. I pummel in and out of her, pounding her pussy with hard strokes. She shudders underneath me, and her cunt spasms, clutching on to me, milking me until I've completely filled her up with my release. My heart's racing, I'm breathless, and I lie down on top of her, still connected. She has her arms and legs around me as if she doesn't want to let me go. But that's just fine. Because I don't want her to let me go either.

11

DYLAN

*W*e talked a lot through the night, we showered together, and after a quick sandwich, we fell back into bed together.

All night I lie next to her, our arms and legs intertwined. Worry starts to creep in, and no matter what I do, I can't make it stop. I'm too old for her. Ten years isn't much of a difference, but when we live in two different worlds it could be. I've seen the evils of people and what it can do. And she's innocent, young, and happy go lucky. I've never even been a part of a family; what if I don't know what to do? She's meant for great things, she deserves them, and I would hate to take that away from her. Her home is here, and mine is over two thousand miles away. There's her brother who trusted me, and I know he never would have sent me if he expected me to act the way I am. All of it is too much, and the burden is heavy on my chest. My brothers, the guys of Ghost team, depend on me. It's a job where I know I make a difference. Can I really give it up? This is all I've ever known.

The more I think about it all, the faster my heart starts to race.

"Hey. Are you okay?" Jenna asks, looking at me from her spot on my chest.

I nod, not knowing how to answer her. There are so many things I should say to her and talk to her about, but that isn't what comes out. "I need you."

She raises up. "You have me."

The corners of my lips raise in a smile. "Prove it."

She smiles back, no doubt remembering last night when she said the same thing to me.

She lifts her naked body up and puts her leg on the other side of me so she's straddling me. The shyness she had last night is long gone. I like to think that I fucked it out of her, showing her exactly how much I love every curve of her body. Already, my cock is hard and thick between us. She leans forward, her hands on my chest as she lifts up. Her hand fists my cock, and she settles over me. I don't know where to look, at her heavy breasts swaying near my face, her thick waist and thighs that I'm squeezing with my hands, or down between my thighs where she's opened herself for me and we connect as one. All of it wells up inside me. I tell myself to take it slowly, but as she lowers herself on me, I lose all sense of reality. I need to release inside her more than I need my next breath.

I lift my hips, meeting her thrust for thrust. She's moving over me, and her soft whimpers bring my urge to have her to another level. With our bodies connected, I roll her on her back and fuck her like there's no tomorrow. We come in a shattering release that has her screaming my name and me grunting into her neck. It's not enough. It will never be enough. The future is unknown, but there's no way I could give her up. I don't know how to say that to her, but I'm hoping she can feel it with every kiss, every thrust, and every spurt of my seed inside her.

Spent, I pull out of her and lie down beside her, pulling her into my arms. She grimaces but tries to cover it up. "I hurt you," I say, and my heart drops.

She shakes her head. "You didn't. My body... well, it was three times."

"Fuck!" I get up from the bed and walk to the bathroom. I clean myself up before returning for Jenna. I have the shower going, and I don't wait for her to get up. I pick her up, and she starts to laugh. "Are we showering?"

"You are." I put her into the shower and start to take care of her. It's what I should have been doing anyway instead of taking her three times in the span of ten hours. I wash her hair and her body. I gently rub between her legs, and when I try to pull away, she holds my hand there. "What about you? Do I get to wash you too?"

"No, because it will end with me deep inside you again."

She looks at me with her big brown eyes almost pleadingly. I'm learning it's almost impossible to tell her no. I drop my hand and take a step back. "I'm going to let you finish. I'm going to get dressed."

She doesn't like it, but she doesn't try to stop me. I pull on my jeans and T-shirt from the night before and pull out my phone. There are texts and missed calls from Bear and John. I know I need to get back to Tennessee, but I hate the thought of leaving Jenna. This is not going to go well. There are things I have to take care of. I can't just desert the team; it could be a matter of life and death.

And I need to talk to John. He's probably not going to forgive me for this, but I need to talk to him, and I need to do it face to face.

With my mind made up, I put on my boots, and I'm lacing them up when Jenna comes out into the living room. Her smile drops instantly as she takes in my fully clothed body and the packed bag on the floor next to the front door. I stand up. "I have to go to Tennessee."

She stumbles and catches herself with a hand on the back of the chair. She looks so cute with her hair up in a towel and her flushed, makeup-free face. "Okaaay."

I search her guarded face and wait for her to ask me to stay or something. But she doesn't. She crosses her arms over her chest and just nods.

"I need to go to Tennessee and talk to John. I may have a mission in a few days."

She takes a deep breath and nods again. "Okay."

I walk toward her. Leaving here is going to be the hardest thing I've ever done, but I don't have a choice. It's on the tip of my tongue to tell her I love her, but I don't. I can't tell her that and then bring myself to walk out the door.

"Take care of yourself while I'm gone." I pull

her toward me for what is supposed to be a hug, but I can't let her go. I hold her so tightly I know I'm hurting her, but she doesn't complain.

I kiss the crown of her head, and without looking back, I grab my bags and walk out the door.

As soon as it shuts, I stop in my tracks. What am I doing? Walking away from the love of my life? I turn to walk back in, but something stops me. I have to be able to tell her something. I need to talk to Nash to see what my options are. I can't give her promises and not be able to keep them. It could take months to train someone new. And I can't just quit either. If something happened to her brother while he was out on a mission, she would never forgive me. No, I'm doing the right thing. Even though it doesn't feel like it. I'll get my life in order, my shit organized, and then we'll be together.

Jenna

I'M BARELY HOLDING it together. I sit on the couch in a daze for who knows how long. He left. He left with no talk about the future... nothing. I gave myself—all of me: my heart, body and soul—last night, and he's gone.

I move through the motions of getting ready, pulling on my yellow Honeybee T-shirt and jeans. I barely remember the ride to the coffee shop, and even though I've managed to hold it together, I fall apart as soon as I see Madison.

She puts the others in charge and shoves me into my office, slamming the door behind us. "Who do I need to kill? Paul?"

I wipe at my tears that I can't seem to stop from falling now. "No, Paul is in jail."

She pushes me into my office chair and drags another one from the corner to sit down in front of me. Her hands grip my shoulders. "Then who? Did something happen with your brother or uh, Dylan?" I tense when she says his name. "That fucker! What did he do?"

I shake my head and sigh. Where do I even start? "He didn't necessarily DO anything."

"Jenna, look at me. What happened? Just the way he looked at you, he thought you hung the moon and stars. I don't understand."

I sit back in my chair and start to think about the night before and this morning. Everything was perfect. Or at least I thought so. So what happened?

"I can see your mind going a thousand miles a minute. Talk to me."

I sigh. "We had s-e-x."

Madison rolls her eyes, no doubt because I spelled it again. Her forehead creases. "Was it awful?"

I jump up from my seat and start to pace the small, confined office. "No, it wasn't awful. It was earth-shattering. I mean, the things he did, Madison, it was everything I ever needed." I turn and face her, holding up three fingers. "Three times. Three times we did it." My face is red, I know it is, but at this point I don't care. If I can't talk about it with Madison, then I can't talk about it with anyone.

She pulls her feet up in the seat. "So what happened?"

I fall back into my seat. "He left."

She jumps up this time. "He left. What? While you were sleeping?"

"No, this morning. I came out of the shower, and his bags were packed. He said he had to go and talk to my brother and he might have a mission in a few days. He hugged me and said... he said, 'Take care of yourself while I'm gone.'" I can't stop shaking my head in confusion. I just don't get it. "How could he just leave?"

Silence fills the tiny space until Madison asks, "Well, did you ask him?"

"No, I didn't ask him. I should have. But I was stunned. We were... intimate right before that. I just don't get it."

"I need coffee. Do you want some coffee? Or I can make you a tea."

I shrug. "Sure, I'll take a coffee too."

Madison walks out of the office, leaving me deep in my thoughts. There's an ache in my heart, and it feels like it's breaking in two. I've never experienced anything like I have in the last twenty-four hours, and I can't help but wonder, *Really, is this it? Is this how it ends? Is he coming back for me?* My stomach starts to hurt just thinking about it.

Madison walks back in, holding two steaming cups of coffee. She hip-checks the door to shut it and hands me my mug before taking her seat again. "Okay, so tell me everything you know about Dylan."

"Uggghhhh. I can't talk about him. Aren't you supposed to be trying to get my mind off him instead?"

She blows on the hot liquid. "No, I want to

figure this out because it doesn't make sense. He doesn't seem like a player."

I shake my head. "He's not."

"Do you think he's married or something?"

I shake my head again. "No. I know he's not."

She nods as if we're getting somewhere. "Okay, how do you know for sure?"

I take a drink of my coffee. It's made perfectly with just the right about of sugar and milk. I set it down on the Honeybee coaster, remembering last night. "Well, he went to take care of all that with Paul, and when he came back, I was a mess worried about him. His knuckles were all messed up, and I don't know, it's like he couldn't believe that I was worried about him. I know my brother and the rest of the team care about him... but I feel like he's never really had someone that cared about him. Does that make sense?"

She holds her hand up. "Wait! He beat up Paul?"

I nod. "Yeah, his hands were pretty messed up. He said he made him pay... that no one messes with his woman and gets away with it."

She uncrosses her legs and stomps a foot on the ground. "He said that?"

I nod.

She's looking at me with a bit of jealousy on her face as she fans herself. "Jenna, give it a day. Two max. He'll be back."

I can't stop the flare of hope that starts to bloom in my chest. "How do you know?"

"Maybe he just needs to get his shit together or something, Jenna. I don't know. But I have no doubt. He's going to come back for you."

I nod, wanting to believe what she's saying but also not wanting to get my hopes up. My phone dings with a message. I pull it out of my pocket and click the screen, and it says I have an email from Seeking Curves. I know I promised my brother, but I'm not even ready to deal with that. I clear the notification and lay my head back on the chair.

"Go home. I have this covered. Go home, take a hot shower, drink some more tea, and relax today."

"Madison, I can't just leave you..."

"We're fine. Story and Roger are here. Take today off."

Maybe Madison's right... maybe I should take the day off... and maybe Dylan will come back for me? If and when he does, he's going to have a lot of explaining to do.

*T*his doesn't feel right. It didn't feel right leaving Jenna. It didn't feel right driving to the airport, and it doesn't feel right sitting in the terminal either. I should have told her things before I left, but like a big dummy, I kept them inside. Maybe it's my compulsive, analytical need to have everything lined up and perfect before acting on something, but whatever it is, it's stupid. I've tried calling her, but she's not answering her phone.

I'm staring at my phone wondering what to do next when it dings with an email, and the notification is from Seeking Curves. It's a dating service that John asked me to check out a while back for him. I never told anyone, but I filled out the application. At the time I told myself it was for research purposes. They guaranteed a hundred percent match, so I wanted to test the theory. But I'd never heard anything from them until today. I should have canceled my membership, but honestly, I forgot all about it.

I open the email to see how to cancel, but the name *Jenna* stands out. I click on the email to open it and scan it quickly. *You have a 100% match. Don't miss your chance with Jenna. Click here to see her profile.* I hold my breath. *It can't be*, I tell myself. I click on the link and instantly an image of Jenna opens up, and my heart stops. How! Jenna—my Jenna—is on Seeking Curves. I jump up from my seat and start to search her profile. Reading, it says that we are a hundred percent match, but I didn't need a matchmaking service to tell me that. I knew it.

But just as quickly as that thought comes, there's another one. There are probably other men right now being matched to her. There could be other men looking at her profile, hoping to ask her for a date. She won't go... it will be over my dead body first.

Frustration takes over, and I open my phone. I hit the speed dial button for John, and when he answers, I start right in. "Remember that Seeking

Curves you asked me to check out? A few weeks ago? Why did you do that?"

"For Jenna. I wanted to help her find someone so I didn't have to worry about her. Why? You said the company was legit and completely safe."

"Fuck!"

John snarls into the phone, "What is it, Riggs? I made Jenna promise to try it out. You better tell me if there's a problem."

My heart is hammering in my chest, and my head is pounding. I had hoped to do this face to face, but I don't have time for that. "She's not using the service. I'm taking her off of it." I grab my bag and turn toward the exit. I still need to talk to Nash, but I'm going to have to do it tomorrow. I can't wait another day for what I need to tell Jenna.

"Uh, what are you talking about? What's happening?"

"I'm her match, John. I'm the only fuckin' match for her. She's not going to be going out with anyone else."

I walk out of the terminal to the line of cabs. I get in the first one I come to and give them the address for Jenna's apartment. John hears me and almost screams into the phone. "That's Jenna's address. I thought you were coming home. What's going on, Riggs? This is my sister we're talking about, and you have around five seconds to explain yourself before I come to California on my own."

I sit back in the seat as the cabbie takes off down the road. We're only around ten minutes from Jenna's apartment, so I need to make this quick. "I came here to protect your sister, and well, I don't know how to say it, but I fell in love with her."

He gasps. "You love her? How is that even possible? You just met her. You don't even know her."

I clench my eyes shut tight. I'm not used to answering to anyone, but I have to take into account that this is Jenna's brother. I can't just tell him to fuck off. "I do know her. I know that she worries about you nonstop. I know she misses being part of a family. I know she has an annoying best friend that will straight-up stab somebody that messes with her. I know she made this little coffee shop into something amazing. She's kind-hearted, would do anything for anyone, and more than anything, she needs someone that will stand with her. Let her be the woman she is and always have her back. That's me, John. I'm that guy."

He barely pauses, and I can hear the smile in his voice when he says, "Okay."

I'm all prepared to keep going, but I'm stumped when he says that. "Okay? Okay you're not going to try and stop me?"

"Riggs, I know you're supposed to be the smart one in the crew, but I'm not dumb. I know you, and I know my sister. Did I warn you to stay away from my sister? No, I didn't. I made you promise to protect her and not to hurt her. That's it. I knew you two were meant for each other."

A warmth spreads through my chest. I thought this was going to be a battle. I thought he'd be mad.

I put my forehead on the seat in front of me. "I need to figure out how to tell Nash. I'll have to train someone."

"What the fuck you talking about now, Riggs?"

"Moving to LA."

"Moving to LA! I swear you're the smartest man I know, but sometimes you're dumb. I didn't put you two together for you to move to LA. You're bringing her to Tennessee."

"But she... her business... she loves it here."

"I know my sister. Talk to her about it and then worry about Nash."

I can't ask her to uproot her whole life for me. I should be the one. I'd follow her anywhere, but he's right: I need to talk to her about this. "Fuck, why didn't I call you before I left her house?"

"I don't know, but you better fix it."

"Riggs, I've always thought of you as a brother. Now we can just make it official." He pauses. "Wait, you do plan on making it official right?"

"Damn straight I do."

"You fuckin' better," John grumbles.

"I gotta go. I'm almost at Jenna's."

"Good luck. And have my sister call me."

I hang up the phone and start digging out my wallet. As soon as the cab pulls into the apartment complex, I throw bills over into the front seat. "Here you go, thanks."

"Good luck, man," he hollers back at me.

I race toward her door, stopping outside to catch my breath and to try and put together my thoughts. I know I want Jenna. Nothing else matters but her. I knock on the door, three swift knocks. Because I'm impatient, I knock again, this time more insistently.

As soon as I stop, I hear Jenna's voice through the door. "What do you want, Dylan?"

I put my hands on the base of the door and am staring at the peephole even though I can't see a damn thing. "I want to talk to you."

I should probably take it down a notch, but I can't. The frantic need to hold her in my arms is strong. I try the door handle, and it doesn't budge.

I can barely hear her through the door, but she says, "What is it? Did you forget something? Go away and I'll mail it to you."

What the fuck? I brace my hands on the door frame, ready to kick it in. "Open the fuckin' door before I break it down."

Fuck. My heart is racing, my hands are sweating, and I start to feel dizzy. The need to hold her, to claim her as my own is all-consuming. I won't fuckin' leave until she's off that matchmaker site and she tells me she's mine. That's it.

I'm about to rear my foot back when I hear the latch, and I know she's unlocking the door. She undoes the two dead bolts but doesn't open the door. I try the handle again, and this time it opens. I walk into the room, my chest rising and falling, and she's across the room with a robe pulled around her and her arms crossed on her chest. She has a vacant look on her face, her eyes red and puffy like she's been crying. I'm across the room in an instant.

But when I reach her, she puts her hand up to stop me, and she moves to the other side, putting the coffee table between us. My voice softens. "I'm sorry. I need you to listen to me."

She laughs, but it's not a haha laugh, it's a disgusted one. "Really. You want to talk now? The time to talk was probably earlier after you fucked me and then couldn't get out of here fast enough. I mean what the heck, Dylan? Now you want me to listen to you? I don't think you have anything I want to hear." Her face is red and got even redder when she said "fucked." I don't think I've heard her cuss before, and the way she stumbles over the word, I don't think she's comfortable with it.

She's still holding her hand up, but I don't care. I'm not having this conversation like this. I lift my leg and step over the coffee table and have my arms around her in an instant. She's struggling, but I don't care. I heft her over my shoulder and carry her down the hall into her bedroom.

She's yelling at me, telling me to put her down, and when I get close to the bed, I do exactly as she asks. I put her down, but before she can get up, I'm on top of her. My hands are on hers, holding them in place over her head. My body is pressed hard against hers, and she can't move. I know she's independent and stubborn, but she's going to listen to me. "Is that what you think we did? We fucked?"

She stops then, and her eyes are staring daggers at me. "What would you call it? I'm pretty sure if you have sex and the man runs away after, that's exactly what it's called."

I lower my head so our faces are only inches apart. "I made love to you, Jenna. We made love is what I call it."

She huffs in frustration, but there's hope in her eyes. "Oh yeah, well, you must have liked it so much you just couldn't wait to get out of here."

"Jenna, please listen to me. I came here to protect you, but from the moment John showed me your picture, I knew. This morning, my mind was a mess. I wanted to do everything right. I was going to talk to John... about us, about how I feel about you."

She juts out her chin. "Don't you think you should tell me how you feel about me first?"

"I love you. I love everything about you. I wasn't thinking right when I left here. I was trying to figure out how to talk to Nash about my job and seeing if I could station here or—"

"In LA?"

I nod. "Yeah, I have a mission in two days that I have to go on, then I'll have to train someone, but then I can move here and—"

I've loosened my hold on her now, and she puts her hands on my chest and pushes. "Wait, let me up."

With jerky movements, I roll off her and sit up. This isn't going how I thought it would. She's about to tell me to go, and I'm not going to be able to. I can't leave her.

She sits beside me and pulls a leg up on the bed to sit sideways and face me. "So let me get this straight. You left here this morning to tell John you love me, and you were going to quit your job... the one you love."

I almost deny loving my job, but I know I'd be lying. "Yes."

"To be with me?"

I shake my head. "I've done this all wrong... I know I have. I should have talked to you before I left. I should have seen how you felt about it all before I started making all these decisions, but Jenna, I didn't even think. I physically can't lose you. If you tell me you don't want to be with me, I'm still moving here just so I can work every day on changing your mind."

"No."

Heat flushes through my body. I can literally feel the vein in my neck vibrating under my skin. I try to tamp down the anger and fear. "That's not an option, Jenna. You're mine."

My whole body is pulled tight. She's searching my face and slides closer to me on the bed. "I can't let you give up your work."

I start to breathe again, but just barely. I won't feel normal again until she tells me she's mine. "I'm not giving you up."

"Dylan—" she starts, but I don't let her finish. "I'm telling you, Jenna, all that matters to me is you. Tell me you're mine, and we can work the rest of it out."

She cups my jaw, her hand going across the stubbled hair of my chin. "I love you too, Dylan Riggs."

My chest heaves with emotion, and all I can get out is "Jenna" before I'm pulling her in my lap. "I'll never walk out again. Never."

Her eyes flutter closed, and when she opens them again, I can see the pain in them. Her arms go tighter around me. "I thought you were leaving me. I thought... I thought you got what you wanted, and you were leaving."

My hands grip her waist in a possessive hold, my fingers digging into her delicate skin. I force myself to loosen my hold. "Jenna, baby, what I want from you is for you to be my wife."

She gasps. And I continue, "I want to live with you, lie with you in my arms every night and wake up like that too. I want you to have my babies. I want to help you make all your dreams come true. I want it all, Jenna. But only with you."

I cup her face and hold her steady, searching her face. "Be mine, Jenna. Be my wife."

"Yes," she answers, nodding her head, tears rolling down her face.

I can't hold back any longer. I press my lips to hers. I've already learned that there's not a simple kiss with Jenna. Once I taste her, once I feel her lips on mine, I want more than just a peck of our lips. I want to ravage her, mark her, and show everyone that she's mine.

I lay her back on the bed and settle over top of her. I want to take her, more than anything, but I know there's something I have to do first.

I pull my lips from hers. "Needless to say, you're going to have to come off Seeking Curves."

She looks confused for a minute and then blushes. "John wanted..."

I shake my head, not needing her to explain. I

pull my phone from my pocket and open the email I got. "I got this."

She scans the email. "Dylan Riggs, are you on Seeking Curves?" Her face is filled with jealousy, and before she can get herself worked up, I tell her, "Yes, I joined when John asked me to check it out. I didn't know you then, but I filled out the application. This is the first match I got."

She stutters. "Me? I'm your first match?"

I shake my head. "No, you're my only match."

I kiss her then, because I can't hold back anymore. I put everything I have into this kiss. The love I feel for her, the fear of losing her, the jealousy when I found out she was on Seeking Curves, all of it. My hand slides down her body, and she stops me, pulling her face away. "So you know this means you're coming off Seeking Curves, right?"

I nod. "Yeah, baby, I know."

Seemingly satisfied, she pulls at my shirt, smiling. "That's good 'cause I don't share."

My shirt comes off my head, and she tosses it to the floor. I pull her robe open, and she's naked underneath. My eyes bulge out of my head, looking at her. She's the most beautiful woman I've ever seen, and I know I'll never get tired of her. "I don't share either." I grunt the words at her.

She reaches between us, her hands quickly undoing the button and zipper on my jeans. I help her pull them down as she takes off the thin robe. I reach between her thighs, and she's already soaked for me. Because I can't wait to claim her, I enter her, hard and fast. With each thrust, she mewls underneath me. I kiss her, pushing in and out of her, claiming her. "You're mine, Jenna."

She meets me thrust for thrust. "Ahhh! And you're mine."

"Open your eyes. Look at me," I tell her.

She does, and the emotion is right there; I can feel the love she has for me. It's too much; I can feel emotion welling up inside me. It's a need to possess her. It's overwhelming, and I try to tamp it down, but I can't. "Fuck! I love you, Jenna."

She opens her mouth, but all that comes out is a strangled cry as her orgasm takes over and her pussy convulses on my dick. I keep thrusting through her tight channel as my balls clench and my climax rocks through me. Deep and low in my throat, I say it again. "Mine."

She stares back at me, satisfied and smug. "Yours."

"What are you doing?" Dylan asks from the bed next to me. I had gotten up to grab my laptop and snuggled back into bed.

I'm reading the email from Seeking Curves, and sure enough, it says that Dylan is my match. I'm in the middle of composing my email, thanking them for their services and telling them they have done a wonderful job with the match. "I'm emailing Seeking Curves, thanking them for the match."

He nuzzles his head against me, kissing my belly where his head is resting. "Okay."

I send the email and open the Seeking Curves website. "Now all I have to do is cancel my profile."

He freezes next to me and raises his head. "You don't have to."

I laugh. "Sure I do. And then right after, you can use my computer to cancel yours."

He clears his throat. "No, I mean you don't have to because I got up in the middle of the night and canceled it for you."

"Uh..." I start.

He sits up in the bed next to me, searching my face. "I couldn't sleep last night. I kept thinking about you getting matched to someone else, so I hacked into the server and closed our profiles."

"Dylan..."

He shrugs his shoulders. "I'm not sorry."

"You'll get caught."

He smirks as if he knows something I don't know. "I won't."

I forget that he's some kind of badass techy mercenary that probably has clearance on anything he wants to access. To me, he's just Dylan. My hard working, possessive man.

"I hate to say it. But I can't just quit my job without notice. I have a mission that I have to get back to Tennessee for."

I nod and take a deep breath. I'm going to

worry, I know I am. But this is who he is. "Okay, and you can't tell me where you're going, right?"

He shakes his head. "No. But as soon as the mission's over, I'm going to talk to Nash about quitting and finding my replacement."

I close my laptop and turn over in the bed to look at him. He reaches for me, but I put my hand on his chest. "We need to talk."

He stops, his brow lowered and eyes blinking, unsure. "About what?"

"Now hear me out."

He's already shaking his head. He sits up in the bed. "I'm not going to like this, I can tell by the way you're starting it."

I get lost staring at his hard chest. He puts a finger under my chin and raises my face up. "Talk to me, honey."

"I want to move to Tennessee. I'm going to let Madison run the shop here for a while until I decide what to do with it. But also, I want you to keep your job. I know it's dangerous, and I'm going to worry about you, but I know what it means to you. Those guys are like your family..."

"You. You're going to be my family," he interrupts me.

I roll my eyes. "I know that, but I'm not letting you give up something you love."

He shakes his head. "So how can I let you give up what you love? Your business that you started from the ground up? Your best friend?" He's still shaking his head.

"First of all, Madison and I have been friends since grade school, so don't be surprised if she follows me to Tennessee. Second of all, I do love the coffee shop, but I'll be honest. I've thought about moving before when John asked me to. If I want to, I can open a shop there. It will all work out how it's supposed to. I just know that I want to build our life together, and I want to do it with you in Tennessee."

He grabs my shoulders. "Are you sure about this? I don't want you to regret this or resent me..."

I'm already shaking my head. "I won't. I could never."

He puts his hand around the base of my neck and searches my eyes. I'm completely vulnerable, letting him see the love shining in my eyes for him. "I'm going to show you every day how much I love you, Jenna. You'll never go a day without knowing how much you mean to me. I'm going to work hard to give you everything you want."

I curl into his chest. "You. That's all I want."

His chest swells underneath my head, and I know it's his heart reacting to how much I love this man. "Done," he murmurs. And in his arms, held against his chest, I feel more loved, safer, and more cherished than I've ever felt in my life. There's a giddiness I feel, excited about what our future holds.

EPILOGUE 2
DYLAN

One Year Later

I stand on Main Street looking up and down the street. I never thought I'd be happy living in a small town, but now that Jenna is here in Whiskey Run, there's nowhere else I'd want to be. There's a lot that has happened in one year. Jenna hired someone to run her store in LA. We got married. We got pregnant. And now we're opening a second Honeybee in Whiskey Run.

I'm staring up at the big yellow sign with the honeybee logo just as my wife comes out of the door with a hand over her belly. I rush toward her and pull her into my arms. "So are you happy?"

She laughs. "How can I not be?"

I drop down into a squat and kiss Jenna's belly. "What about you, little guy? You happy?"

Jenna groans, and her hand goes to the side of her stomach. "You know anytime you talk to him he kicks me, right?"

I raise up and pull her into my arms. "I'm sorry."

She laughs again. "No you're not. But I'm not mad about it."

"Really! Really, we have a shop to open in three days, and I can't get anything done because you two are always making out," Madison hollers from the open front door of Honeybee. Jenna was right. She called it that Madison would move to Tennessee and follow her. I don't think Jenna is the only reason she moved here, but I'll save that story for another day.

I lean my head against Jenna's. "So your friend is trying to cock block me."

Jenna smiles up at me. She does that a lot these days. She's always smiling, and it's in that smile that lets me know we made the right decision when we moved here to Tennessee. She loves this place... and everyone loves her. I still go a little crazy sometimes, especially when I see someone admiring my wife. I've been known to go a little crazy over her, but luckily, Whiskey Run is a small town, and it seems everyone knows she's mine. I don't know anyone stupid enough to go against my friends and me. That's one good thing about being stationed in a small town.

"So what about you?" Jenna asks.

I put my arm around her shoulder and walk her toward the awning to get her out of the sun. "What about me?" I ask her.

She stops and grips the front of my shirt with both her hands. "Are you happy?" She's serious when she asks me, and I can't help but wonder if I'm not doing something right. She has to know how happy she makes me. "Yes, I'm happy. You make me happy."

She pulls me in for a kiss just as my phone goes off. I hate to, but I have to answer it. "This is Riggs."

"Wheels up in thirty."

My body tenses when I hear Nash's voice on the other end and can tell he's on edge. My commander never lets anything get to him, and knowing that something has put this in his voice lets me know it's something bad. "I'll be ready. Anything I need to know?"

Jenna holds me tighter as I listen on the phone. "Yeah, Riggs. It's Brooklyn. She was kidnapped."

"Brooklyn!" It's like a sucker punch to my stomach. Brook is like one of us. She's Walker's secretary, and she's always around headquarters. Whoever it is that came for Brook, they came for all of us. "I'll see you soon," I say and hang up the phone.

"Someone has Brook?" Jenna asks.

"Yeah, honey. I have to go. I love you."

She nods. "I know. I love you too."

I bellow for Madison, and she sticks her head out the door. "Code Blue, Madison."

Worry fills her eyes. We made this up when I go on missions. She's to help look out for Jenna now that she's pregnant. "I got her," she says, and I have no doubt she does.

Jenna's still holding on to me. "I don't want to let you go."

I kiss her, committing her taste to memory. "I know. But I have to go. I'll be back as soon as I can. I love you, baby."

With one last kiss, I turn to go. Jenna's echo, telling me she loves me too, follows me to my car.

I'm so excited to bring you the
alpha mercenaries of Whiskey Run.
Get ready for Walker's story in Ransom.
Get it here: mybook.to/RansomHopeFord

FREE BOOKS

Want FREE BOOKS?
Go to www.authorhopeford.com/freebies

JOIN ME!

JOIN MY NEWSLETTER & READERS GROUP

www.AuthorHopeFord.com/Subscribe

JOIN MY READERS GROUP ON FACEBOOK

www.FB.com/groups/hopeford

Find Hope Ford at www.authorhopeford.com

ABOUT THE AUTHOR

USA Today Bestselling Author Hope Ford writes short, steamy, sweet romances. She loves tattooed, alpha men, instant love stories, and ALWAYS happily ever afters. She has over 100 books and they are all available on Amazon.

To find me on Pinterest, Instagram, Facebook, Goodreads, and more:

www.AuthorHopeFord.com/follow-me

Printed in Great Britain
by Amazon